tempted

RECKLESS MC OPEY TEXAS CHAPTER

WALL STREET JOURNAL & USA TODAY BESTSELLING AUTHOR

KB WINTERS

Copyright and Disclaimer

This book is a work of fiction. The names, characters, places and incidents are products of the writer's imagination and have been used fictitiously and are not to be construed as real. Any resemblance to persons, living or dead, actual events, locales or organizations is entirely coincidental.

Copyright © 2019 Book Boyfriends Publishing

All rights reserved. No part of this publication may be reproduced, stored in or introduced into a retrieval system, or transmitted, in any form, or by any means (electronic, mechanical, photocopying, recording, or otherwise) without the prior written permission of the copyright owner. The author acknowledges the trademarked status and trademark owners of various products referenced in this work of fiction, which have been used without permission. The publication/use of the trademarks is not authorized, associated with, or sponsored by the trademark owners.

Table of Contents

Copyright and Disclaimer ii
Chapter One 7
Chapter Two 15
Chapter Three 25
Chapter Four 45
Chapter Five 55
Chapter Six 65
Chapter Seven 79
Chapter Eight 87
Chapter Nine 91
Chapter Ten.. 109
Chapter Eleven 115
Chapter Twelve 135
Chapter Thirteen 145
Chapter Fourteen 161
Chapter Fifteen 185
Chapter Sixteen 195
Chapter Seventeen 203
Chapter Eighteen 223
Chapter Nineteen 235

Chapter Twenty	243
Chapter Twenty-One	253
Chapter Twenty-Two	267
Chapter Twenty-Three	281
Chapter Twenty-Four	291
Chapter Twenty-Five	299
Chapter Twenty-Six	309
Chapter Twenty-Seven	319
Chapter Twenty-Eight	329
Chapter Twenty-Nine	345
Chapter Thirty	353
Chapter Thirty-One	365
Chapter Thirty-Two	375
Chapter Thirty-Three	385
Chapter Thirty-Four	397
Epilogue	411

TEMPTED

Reckless MC Opey Texas Chapter

By Wall Street Journal & USA Today Bestselling Author

KB Winters

Chapter One

Gunnar

"We're gonna be cowboys!"

Maisie had been singing that song since we got on the interstate and left Nevada and the only family we'd had in the world behind. For good. Cross was my oldest friend, and I'd miss him the most, even though I knew we'd never lose touch. I'd miss Jag too, even Golden Boy and Max. The prospects were cool, but I had no attachment to them. Though I gave him a lot of shit, I knew I'd even miss Stitch. A little. It didn't matter that the last year had been filled with more shit than gold, or that I was leaving Vegas in the dust, we were all closer for the hell we'd been through.

But still, I was leaving.

Maisie and I'd been on the road for a couple of days. Traveling with a small child took a long damn time. Between bathroom breaks and snack times we'd be lucky to make it to Opey by the end of the month.

Lucky for me, Maisie had her mind set on us becoming cowboys, complete with ten gallon hats, spurs and chaps, so she hadn't shed one tear, *yet*. It wasn't something I'd been hoping for, but I was waiting patiently for reality to sink in and the uncontrollable sobs that had a way of breaking a grown man's heart.

"You're not a boy," I told her and smiled through the rear view mirror. "Hard to be a cowboy if you're not even a boy."

Maisie grinned, a full row of bright white baby teeth shining back at me right along with sapphire blue eyes and hair so black it looked to be painted on with ink.

"I'm gonna be a cow*girl* then! A cowgirl!" She went on and on for what felt like forever, in only the way that a four-year-old could, about all the cool cowgirl stuff she'd have. "Boots and a pony too!"

"A pony? You can't even tie your shoes or clean up your toys and you want a pony?"

She nodded in that exaggerated way little kids did. "I'll learn," she said with the certainty of a know it all teenager, a thought that terrified the hell out of me. "You'll help me, Gunny!"

Her words brought a smile to my face even though I hated that fucking nickname she'd picked up from a woman I refused to think about ever again. I'd help Maisie because that's what family did. Hell, she was the reason I'd uprooted my entire fucking life and headed to the great unknown wilds of Texas. To give Maisie a normal life or as close to normal as I was capable of giving her. "I'll always help you, Squirt."

"I know. Love you Gunny!"

"Love you too, Cowgirl." I winked in the mirror and her face lit up with happiness. It was the pure joy on her face, putting a bloom in her cheeks that convinced me this was the right thing to do. I didn't want to move to Texas, and I didn't want to live on a goddamn ranch, but that was my future. The property was already bought and paid for with my name on the deed. It was just a few thousand acres, but it was all mine, and I had big plans for the place. If I didn't run back to Cross, Mayhem and the Reckless Bastards before I got it off the ground.

"Gunny, will I make friends in Texas?"

"Sure you will."

I hoped she would, but what the hell did four-year-old's do all day? "We'll make sure to find you some playmates, I promise. Plus, we'll find you a preschool, okay?"

Before we left, Moon, my Prez's old lady, had given me a list of places that were good to meet up with other parents and arrange playdates for the kids. More information out of my wheelhouse, but I would do anything for my baby sister.

"What about your friends?"

"Hey, don't you worry about me, little girl. I worry about you and that's how things go. All right?" Her stubborn expression was the first hint that I'd have my hands full with this little girl until the day I died. Lips pinched into a frown, face red and scowling, chin tilted up in defiance.

"Gunny is family and family is everything," she said in a sing-song voice I knew she'd gotten from Vivi.

I knew those words though, had heard them plenty from Moon and Vivi, not to mention all the other old ladies in the MC. Women who had stepped in to help with Maisie, loving and caring for her as if she were their own. I owed them a debt I could never repay so all I could do was keep moving forward and make sure Maisie's life was better than mine.

"That's right but you're too young to worry. You have all the time in the world to worry about me and everyone else. For now, enjoy being a kid."

"I'm not a kid, I'm a cowgirl!"

"Not yet."

The closer we got to Texas the more the doubts and the fear crept in, which was bullshit. I didn't do doubt, and I sure as hell didn't do fear, at least not until

I became a father to my baby sister. Taking care of Maisie had given me a new appreciation for everything my mom had gone through. From her addiction to the bottle to her never ending search for the elusive Mr. Right, all with the constant weight and fear of a tiny little person who needed her. For everything.

In the three years since our mother had passed, my feelings had softened toward her. I did my best to give Maisie good memories of the woman who'd given us matching blue eyes. I would make sure she knew her mother and also knew that she was the reason Maisie had a shot at normal. It was her final act and one borne of complete selflessness, which meant I would do everything in my power to make sure I did it right.

A quick look in the mirror told me what the silence had already confirmed, Maisie had fallen asleep.

In the silence of the truck my thoughts inevitably drifted back to Mayhem. The Reckless Bastards. Leaving had been hard, harder than the decision to leave the Army. Hell it was harder than deciding to *join* the Army. And the Rangers. "But it's done."

Saying it out loud helped. Made it seem final. Which I guessed it was.

We pulled into the ranch as the sun began to set and a calm settled over me. There was a long damn road ahead, and I was guaranteed to make more than my share of mistakes, but somehow, I knew this was the right choice.

For both of us.

KB WINTERS

Chapter Two

Peaches

"Ouch, shit!"

Stumbling around my New York apartment on a twisted ankle wasn't exactly how I pictured spending my Friday night. Then again, I hadn't planned on someone trying to snuff me out either. Yet here I was, burning another apartment. Not burning in the pyro sense of the word, just getting rid of all traces of me inside this residence.

My soon-to-be *former* residence and all because of a job I never should have fucking said yes to in the first place. Now, MiB types in suits tried to put tracking devices on my car, my bicycle, and even my jacket in the subway this morning. But that wasn't all. I had thugged-out men stalking me with their carefully placed prison tats mingled in with the colorful and expensive body art if I knew where to look. And I, unfortunately, lived a life that meant I knew exactly where to look.

It was that life that led me to a career as a government contractor via a short stint as a poorly paid lackey for said government. The Feds caught me using my foster family's shitty wi-fi for things I shouldn't have. Work for us now, they said, or it's jail time for you. It was a rookie mistake, and I hadn't made one like that since.

Now I'd made much bigger mistakes with higher stakes than juvie. As a paid hacker for the good ol' U.S. government, I saw some shit I shouldn't have and now all kinds of bad guys were on my tail.

With my eye on the clock, I went through the whole place, taking down my framed photos and replacing them with pictures of strangers. People who had no connection to me. Storage units and estate sales were great places to get real photos of real people, and I had plenty of them stacked in boxes for just this kind of emergency, another thing this life had taught me. I was in phase one of my exit strategy. The shit had hit the proverbial fan and splattered everywhere, so I was getting the fuck out of Dodge.

A few hours later, I'd made sure I'd thoroughly burned the apartment. I'd packed up all of my emergency cash and IDs, personal mementos, and hidden USBs, and in their place, I'd set special equipment that would infect, fry and distort any and all data on them and any device attempting to connect or sync with it. When the place was fully burned and looking totally spotless and unlived in, I grabbed my stuff and left through the back service entrance.

Everything had turned into one big clusterfuck and it was my own goddamn fault. When Bob pulled Vivi in for some *mandatory* work in order to keep her man and his club out of prison, I should have hung up my keyboard then. The writing was on the wall but I'd been too arrogant to see it, or maybe I was stupid enough to think I could keep it up forever and none of the bad shit would ever touch me.

"Look at me now, covered in bad shit." Literally and figuratively. Ever since I'd said yes when Bob approached me for this fucking job, it'd been the bane of my existence.

Yeah, it padded my bank account nicely but what the fuck difference did that make if I couldn't sleep in my five thousand square foot New York City apartment, or live in it?

The truth was, I took the job for the same reason I stayed in this line of work even after the government tried to sink their claws into me, because the money was too fucking good to pass up for a gutter rat like me. Foster care taught me one thing, survival.

In this world, money pretty much guaranteed it so I'd said yes. And now all I had was a bunch of electronic equipment as I made my way from the Upper West Side up to Brooklyn where one of my well-seasoned aliases rented a crappy studio apartment.

I rushed over there to pick up a few clothes, more cash and a quick scrub. I ran into an old friend on the front stoop.

"Hey, Wallace." He was an old homeless man who took advantage of the fact that I hardly ever went to the second floor studio apartment, which was located above a massage parlor, nail salon, and dry cleaners. Sometimes, I'd let him use it to stay warm and dry overnight.

"Hey girl! I'd ask how you are but I think I already know." His smile was wide but his words confused me.

"What do you mean?" I asked him.

He stood up from the bus bench, and God bless him, but he needed a shower. Bad. "I saw them spies sneak in earlier and tear the place up. Had the grace of a bull in a china shop!"

I didn't want to offend the poor homeless man, but I had to step back. The stench was real. "Did they say anything? Did you?"

He smiled a toothy grin, "Naw. They tore up the place and left. Been a while ago. At least a week. If they come back, I'll tell 'em I ain't seen ya."

I entered the building, pulled my piece out of my bag, and climbed up the flight of stairs. The overhead motion light was broken and the door was open. Not kicked in either, just open. I pushed the door slowly; my piece out front, ready to shoot. A girl could never be too careful.

"Shit." They'd already been here and tossed the place. Luckily, I'd left nothing here to find other than twenty grand I kept in a loose floorboard under the bed. I found it still there, so I shoved it in my bag with my gun and turned back to the door, leaving a few hundred-dollar bills on the table for Wallace.

"Everything all right, girl?" he asked when I saw him outside again.

"It will be. Hey, I won't be back here, ever."

"Figured," he mumbled.

"The lease expires at the end of next month. You can stay here until then if you want. There's some body wash in there. You look like you could use a hot shower."

He blinked. Shocked at first but a slow smile spread across his face, his smile bright, despite all the other signs of his life on the street, rugged skin the color of dirt, God only knew what under his fingernails and his layers of clothes. "I sure could. And you be careful out there."

"Thanks, Wallace. Stay safe now."

"You too," he said with a grin and picked up a few dirty blankets on the sidewalk next to him. "Thanks for the pad. I really appreciate it."

I've been made to sign hella NDA's to make sure I never told a soul about any of the operations I was involved in, too. I never told anyone that certain *agencies* who had no domestic authority operated within the boundaries of their country, and I wouldn't start now. This was seriously dangerous shit, and I would never put anyone I cared about at risk by telling the Feds anything. Certainly not Wallace.

But my morals and ethics and all the shit I thought didn't matter because I operated behind a computer screen—not with guns or bombs—mattered. And it was all because of the fucking CAD. The Covert Affairs Division was *technically* part of the Department of Defense, but the truth was, they operated in a gray area that most people tended to overlook since 9/11, using plenty of contractors like me as well as foreign agents and mercenaries. Most of CAD was made up of current and former military from damn near every U.S. ally in the world. And now they were after me.

I'd do my best to stay one step ahead of the fuckers out to get me. But first, I had to go to the last place I wanted to ever set foot in again. Jersey. I hadn't been back since I left to pay off my debt to the government. Too many fucking memories there for me. Made it hard to think straight. I needed to focus more than I needed anything else right now.

Except for what was in the safe deposit box at First Constitution Bank under a name that only a handful of people knew. And two of those people were dead.

I'd get inside first thing tomorrow, and then I'd disappear for as long as I needed to.

Chapter Three

Gunnar

"Coffee and breakfast are already on the table," Martha Bennett shouted from the kitchen. She was an angel. A saint. A lifesaver. She was the first person I'd hired because nothing else could happen unless I had someone to look after Maisie.

"Thanks, Miss Martha, I'm starving," I called from the bedroom. The scent of bacon and coffee had pulled me straight from bed, got me through a quick shower, and helped me get an energetic four-year-old dressed for the day.

"Yeah, thanks Miss Martha!" Maisie beamed, dashing to her seat at the table, a smile at the older woman with kind eyes and a weakness for military men.

"You are very welcome sweetheart. I hope you like biscuits."

"I do! I love them, right Gunny?" Big blue eyes stared up at me, and I confirmed her words.

"She doesn't just love 'em, Miss Martha, you'll have to keep an eye on her because this little cowgirl will eat all the biscuits on the table."

Maisie giggled when I tickled her, bending all the way over my arm as her little body shook with laughter.

Martha laughed along with us, a load of laundry in her hands. "What an adorable little cowgirl she is," the older woman cooed and pinched Maisie's pink cheeks. "I just need to get these sheets on the line, and I'll come help with breakfast."

"No need Miss Martha, Maisie and I can manage to get the food into our bellies." She insisted on pulling double duty as the nanny and cook, while her daughters were tasked with keeping the house and bunkhouse clean.

"Nonsense. It's been far too long since I've been around a sweet little girl. I admit to being a little bit excited." Her cheeks turned a pretty shade of pink, giving her the charm of a woman half her age.

Martha rushed off while Maisie and I followed the scent of bacon. And coffee. "Wow, look at this spread Maze." I didn't know how the table held up with all the food Martha had prepared. Scrambled eggs, grits, bacon *and* sausage, biscuits, pancakes, fruit, coffee and fresh butter. "Miss Martha you've outdone yourself." Martha's laugh sounded from the laundry room just as the back door smacked open and slammed against the wall. Two younger women walked in, far too dressed up to be Martha's daughters. "Who the hell are you?"

They were both young and blonde and had identical faces. The one in dark jeans stepped forward and crossed her arms. "We work here, who are you?"

"I own this ranch now and you don't just slam in here like a bunch of animals. Now tell me who the hell you are or get out." I didn't normally talk to women like that but we were in a new place and Maisie was my top priority. Always. And I wasn't going to have any woman smart mouthing around her.

The one in the light jeans sauntered toward me, looking just as snooty and defiant as her twin. But clearly, she was the smart one. "I'm Adrian and this is Evelyn. Martha is our mom. She works here, you know?"

Fuck my fucking life sideways and without lube. "Then explain to me why Martha is doing laundry when that is not her job?"

Evelyn yawned and looked down at her nails, a pointed effort to let me know she wasn't intimidated by me. Big mistake on her part. "Ma doesn't mind."

"I mind. She has a job, two of them in fact. And if you want to keep yours, I better not see or hear Martha doing any of your work. Got it?"

Evelyn opened her mouth to argue but Adrian put a hand to her shoulder. "Ma always pitches in but we'll talk to her. It's not like we have anything else to do around here anyway." Despite their bitter words and nasty demeanor, both twins managed to slowly push their tits out in my direction while offering the best pout their lips could manage.

"Martha has plenty to do, and if you don't have enough then maybe the job only requires one of you." I hired them sight unseen because of Martha, but if they weren't up for the job, I'd replace them. Hell with those shitty attitudes. It might make my life easier if they were gone.

"What*ever*." They spoke at the same time, crossing their arms at the same time with the identical defiant chin lift.

These girls thought they were tough, probably because Martha and everyone else let them get away with being total bitches. That changed now. "Get to work."

Both of them turned on the heels of their red and turquoise cowboy boots and stomped off. With an extra swing in their hips. Of course.

A few minutes later Martha arrived back in the kitchen, all smiles. "I see you met my girls."

"I did." And they weren't as impressive as she seemed to think. "Look Martha, I hired you mostly to look after Maisie, but if you're going to do Adrian and Evelyn's work I'll need to reconsider."

"Oh nonsense, I was just—"

"—Martha, stop. Maisie is what I care about most and that's why I hired you. To look after and care for her when I can't. How can you cook for a full ranch, take care of Maisie and do their housekeeping work?"

"It was just a little laundry, Gunnar."

"Then explain to me exactly why I need them both to be here?" I may look like a dumb son of a bitch, but I wasn't and I wouldn't let these snot-nosed cowgirls try to get one over on me. "Either they do their jobs or I have to let them go, Martha."

She wasn't happy but she nodded her agreement. "Maybe I do spoil them too much, but things have been so hard since we lost Colby." I'd heard all about her son who'd died fighting over in Afghanistan and how hard it had hit the Bennett women. "I just want the girls to have a purpose."

That wasn't any of my business. "I just want to make sure Maisie is looked after properly."

"She will be Gunnar, don't you worry."

I gave a short nod and dug into the delicious food on the table. "Thanks and this food looks and tastes incredible, by the way." If I ate like this every single day, I'd definitely have a spare tire by the end of the year.

"I'm glad you like it. I wasn't sure if you'd approve of a hearty Texas breakfast."

"Well I do, Miss Martha. I damn sure do." She smiled and busied herself helping Maisie avoid getting more of her breakfast on her shirt than in her mouth, the funniest and most challenging part of mealtime.

Once breakfast was over, it was time to get down to business. Ranch business. That meant I needed to get off my ass and go meet with my ranch manager.

"You meeting with Holden?" Miss Martha asked as she cleaned up.

"The very one," I said. Holden Jennings was what people in these parts called a good ol' southern boy, meaning he was born and bred in Texas. Add in a stint in the military and he was as Texas as they came.

"Take him a plate if you don't mind," she said.

I didn't mind at all. I took the plate full of food and made my way outside into the bright early morning sun. The temperature hadn't caught up with the sun's impact on the day, but I knew it would. Shielding my eyes with my free hand, I stole a moment to look over the property. It was expansive as fuck and with the sun lighting up the sky in vibrant shades of orange and red and gold. It was beautiful and best of all, it was all mine.

But still, none of it felt like home.

"Morning, sir," Holden said as he greeted me in on the front porch of the house. He was a beast of man, just six feet tall but he was imposing. Probably even intimidating to some with dark brown hair and eyes so dark they looked like two black marbles. But there was no anger or sadness coming from the loose-legged ranch manager, just a casual coolness that instantly put me at ease.

"Call me Gunnar," I said and held out the plate and he took it and sat down on the top step.

"Thank you, Gunnar," he said cracking a wide smile. He took a bite of biscuit and talked with his mouth full. "Last guy who owned this spread preferred to keep things formal. Kind of a dick if you ask me."

He finished off his food in about thirty seconds flat and set the plate on the front porch and wiped his hands on his jeans before shaking my hand. "I prefer Holden," he said in his thick Texas drawl. "Mr. Jennings makes me think of my old man."

He raked a hand through thick hair that bounced right back into place before he covered it with a well-worn cowboy hat. "Wanna take a look around?"

I gave him a nod and followed him to the building closest to the main house. "Smells like horses."

Holden flashed a smile over his shoulder. "This is where we keep 'em. Close to the main house and the bunkhouse, otherwise we'd spend most of our time walking to get to a horse to ride around the property."

I held in a groan at the thought of mounting a fucking horse every day. I could do it; I just wasn't sure I wanted to. Or wanted Maisie up on one. "What about ATVs? Or bikes? You ride?"

Holden smiled again, looking like nothing ever phased him. "Yup. We got a few of those too, but we keep 'em in the barn up over that hill. Mostly for when we need to spend time on the other side of the property. It's a hike."

He had answers for everything. "Why in the hell is this stable blue?"

Holden burst out laughing, smacking his thigh with his hat. "That was the previous owner's Missus. Thought red was too bright this close to the house. I think after a few days of looking at it, you might agree."

I didn't give a shit what color the stables or the barn were. The only thing I cared about was the structure being built on the other end of the property. The rest was just a distraction.

"What else?" If Holden was fazed by my tone, he didn't let on, and I appreciated that. I didn't have time for whiny ass workers. I needed men who could work and more importantly who *wanted* to work. In fact, I didn't care at all about the business of the ranch. Not yet. When I'd bought the ranch, I didn't give much thought to it since Holden had been more than willing to stay on in the same role. Now I wished I'd paid a bit more attention.

"You don't have to worry about keeping things runnin' on the ranch. I've been doing it for years and you can take a look at the weekly reports I gave the old owner, though I know he didn't bother to look at 'em. He was more of the *gentleman* rancher type if you know what I mean."

I knew exactly what he meant, but I also knew I wasn't so different from the last guy. "I want the ranch to be profitable, Holden, but I don't want cows and horses to take up all of my time. If I have questions, I expect prompt answers, otherwise weekly reports are fine."

"Sounds good. I have to get going on some of the chores for the day, but holler if you need anything, and we can set up a time to meet to go over the books whenever you want."

I frowned. "You're the bookkeeper too?"

"Not by choice or by trade, but by default." His grin spread wide to show there were no hard feelings, but I knew the man had to be overworked.

"Let's do the books sooner rather than later and maybe you can recommend a bookkeeper or accountant." Keeping an eye on the books was another damn thing that needed to be done, and at the moment, the job fell in my lap. There wasn't enough time in the day for me to handle all the shit that needed to be dealt with while looking into my own pet project. Never mind dealing with all the new personalities about to descend on the ranch.

"Sounds good, Boss. See ya 'round."

I waved off Holden, happy to see that so far, half of my staff was capable and trouble free. The rest of the guys would trickle in over the next few days. I'd been contacting them for weeks, others heard about my plan and reached out to me. All of them vets, some might call them wounded warriors. Oh, they were all sound in body, more than capable of handling the heavy work on the ranch and the entertainment complex I envisioned. But more than that, I was offering them a place to heal from their war wounds, the scars that didn't show on the surface, the ones that lead to our unacceptable suicide rates and drug use that some had turned to cope with what they'd seen. While I was envisioning a second chance for everyone, I still needed workers and hoped they were more like Holden and Martha than the young twins because this was my sister's future. Her chance at normal. And I would move heaven and hell to make sure she had it. And I would fucking blast through anyone who got between me and that goal.

***

I never thought I would be the kind of guy to sit on a porch and drink coffee while watching the sky change from dawn to morning, but here I was, just a few days in. Up before the damn sun, waiting impatiently for her to bathe the land, *my land*, in splashes of color and light. But nature was just what I needed. I wasn't sure if moving to Texas had been a stroke of genius or the worst goddamn decision I'd ever made.

Only time would tell. I had to move forward, one step at a time until everything was finished. Even though I felt I owed her nothing, I had promised my mother I'd care for her baby. And the minute I held Maisie in my arms I knew I'd do whatever she asked. Even if it was the biggest ask in the fucking world.

"Look after Maisie. Give her the life I was too fucked up to give you. Please."

I wanted to hate her for putting that on me, for transforming my life without a thought of what it meant for me. It would've been pointless anyway. My mother was dying back then. She'd never given a single damn thought to anything besides indulging in booze, drugs and the wrong types of men. Losers. All my life. Just like the old man I never knew. Maisie's dad was some dealer or john Mom used to get high with one more time.

One last time.

No point thinking about that, I reasoned, tossing the rest of my cold coffee over the railing. I walked into the kitchen briefly to refill my mug and stepped outside again, going over my plans for Hardtail Ranch. It had a name but still no purpose. Yet.

On the long drive down to Texas, thinking about what I'd left behind, my brothers, the Reckless Bastards, I got the idea for another group of men to be what they'd been for me. Every Reckless Bastard had served his country with honor, an honor that left each of us bitter and scarred and wary of things like "the greater good." But the club had saved my life and given me direction. A family. It had saved each and every one of us and maybe Hardtail Ranch could be that as well.

A welcoming place for veterans who felt displaced, out of sorts and unsure how to readjust to civilian life. It might be through working with Holden on the ranch side of the business or maybe it'd be at the club. Maybe it'd be something else altogether, but Hardtail Ranch could be our clubhouse. Our home. Our own MC.

"Shit," I said to the rising sun. That was a big vision. It required more than a just a dream. I had to push it down the list for now because first the ranch had to get some cash rolling in and then maybe, Reckless Bastards MC, Opey, Texas Chapter could become a reality.

I let out a long breath at that thought. It was a big mistake. Hell, I'd left Mayhem to keep Maisie safe, but here I was, thinking about another chapter. But bikes were a part of me. In my blood. My DNA. And yet, I scoffed at the thought. What was I thinking, bringing an MC down to Texas? I knew with more certainty than I knew anything else that Hardtail Ranch would be a home for Maisie and me. Filled with family and good times.

I finished my coffee before it got cold and went back inside to get a baseball cap because the Texas sun was no damn joke. I had a long ride to get to the other side of the property. Holden had promised to prioritize repairs on at least one of the ATVs so I could stop playing cowboy on a damn horse.

When I walked into the barn and spotted her, I had to stop for a look. She was a beauty though, a black and white painted horse that was only nice when she wanted food or a cuddle. Other times she was a snob and that was fine, Sassy got me where I needed to go, and I made sure someone cleaned her and cooled her down when I was done. It was the perfect relationship.

When I finally set eyes on my pride and fucking joy, the future home of my adult entertainment club. At least the bones of it for now. I felt my first genuine smile about up and moving to Opey. The foundation was poured and the frame was up but I expected more progress by now. Mostly I envisioned making money from memberships, but I'd welcome the drop in visitors as well. It would be first class all the way, if the assholes I'd hired ever got to work getting the damn thing built.

"Goddammit," I muttered as I looked around for a warm body.

Inside I found exactly who I was looking for. Joplin Saint. The ex-Marine I'd hired to manage The Barn Door, the most exclusive adult playground in all of Texas. It would be members only. A fancy-schmancy place where grown up folks would come to play when they wanted to play dirty. And it was far enough away from the house, Maisie wouldn't be affected. Except for all the money it would bring in.

"Gunnar, right?" He looked right at me but his gaze somehow managed to miss mine completely and my suspicion rose.

"Yeah. Joplin?"

He nodded and accepted my hand in a good, strong handshake. For a Marine. "Yes, sir, but everybody calls me Saint." Again, his posture was straight enough to impress any drill sergeant, but his eyes still wouldn't meet mine.

"Saint, why the fuck does my club have no walls?"

The guy recoiled when I asked and took a step back to stroke his overgrown beard. "The foreman broke his leg and the crew came for two days but they didn't get shit done and then they brought a twelve-pack on the second day. I told them if that's how they worked then stay the fuck away until their foreman was here. I've already sent the vendor a chargeback for the damage they did those two days."

He might have been a little pussy, but it looked like Saint wasn't a man to fuck with. "Good job. Great. Thanks." I looked around and could see The Barn Door come to my life before my eyes. There was no red carpet and no leather benches with brass accents yet, but I could see it all. So clearly.

"If the foreman can't make it back before the week is up, tell the contractor we need someone else or the contract is void."

"Will do, sir."

I froze at what would become the black leather entrance to the club, complete with black and red lights that trained the eye right on the stage where guests were welcome to perform any sensual acts they desired. Alone, together or even in a group. All kinks were welcome. "Saint, we're not in the military anymore. Call me Gunnar. I might even answer to Boss."

A faint smile touched his lips and he nodded. "Copy that, Boss."

I didn't know his story, but I had a feeling that despite first impressions, Joplin Saint might end up becoming family.

Either that or moving to Texas had turned me into a weak-assed pussy in need of a good ass whooping.

Chapter Four

Peaches

I sat inside one of the private event rooms inside Honky Tonk Sushi, a country & western themed sushi bar, waiting for my best friend Vivi to show up. She was already ten minutes late, which was unlike her. I began to worry. If she didn't show up in two and a half minutes, I'd get the fuck out of Vegas to make sure my shit stayed as far away from her as possible.

It was unnerving listening to old ass country songs with a Japanese flair inside a room that was equal parts samurai dungeon and barn, with katana swords on the brick walls, hay on the ground and chopsticks with state flags waving from the tops.

It felt like a normal Wednesday afternoon, best friends meeting up to enjoy a long lunch complete with sake and sushi, but it wasn't. Even the steaming hot miso soup in front of me could do nothing to quell the nausea in my gut or the worry that prickled at the goosebumps on my skin. Somehow, I'd made it from the east coast to Nevada in one piece, but it had been the most stressful three and a half days of my life.

Thousands of miles, a beat up old Cadillac from the early nineties and a lot of night driving left me exhausted, half-blind and delirious, but at least I was here and I was safe. Hopefully, Vivi would have a hideout for me.

With less than thirty seconds to spare Vivi breezed into the room with shoulder length hot pink hair with platinum blonde bangs. And a big ass diamond on her finger.

"Please tell me you guys did a jewelry heist for your honeymoon because that is one giant glacier you're lugging around."

Vivi grinned wide and wiggled her short black nails, which somehow only made the diamond sparkle even more. "Nah, Jag felt like the old ring wasn't sending enough of a message so he upgraded."

I let out a low whistle and looked at my friend carefully. Her smooth pale skin damn near glowed, making me wonder if it was more than love that had her looking so fantastic. "That'll do it." I stood up to give her a proper greeting and wrapped Vivi in my arms tight, hanging on a little longer than I should have because I didn't know when I'd ever get to see her again. "Love looks good on you, chica."

"Thanks, but you didn't ask me to meet in a private room in the middle of the day for a state of the union check-in."

That was the problem with having a friend who knew me so well, it was impossible to bullshit her. "No, I didn't. I'm in some deep shit, the kind where bullets fly at me constantly and without warning. The kind I can't talk about in too much detail."

I hoped I wouldn't give her any of the details, but it wouldn't take long before suits or thugs rolled into Mayhem or Vegas in search of me. "A CAD mission gone wrong. A Paris suburb to target a *possible* American citizen for assassination. Somehow the footage ended up in a batch of data sent to me and the others on the team. They're all dead now."

"Dead? Seriously?"

I nodded; my expression unchanged. "One died in a single car accident on a residential street. Matrix had a heart attack. She was only twenty-two fucking years old, Vivi. A goddamn heart attack. And the CIA liaison has disappeared but it's probably safe to assume he's dead as well."

She let out a low whistle, which just about summed up how I felt about all of this.

"Damn girl when you do trouble, you don't take it easy do ya?"

I shrugged. "There's a hit on me, Vivi. Whatever happened to that liaison, there is a hit out on me, too. Even if I hadn't seen it with my own eyes on the dark web, I found two trackers on my car in the city, one of my aliases was burnt in the process, oh and some stupid asshole shot at me."

Thinking about that again made me sick to my stomach and instinctively I shoved a spoonful of soup in my mouth and moaned, "So good."

Vivi knew what I was doing and arched a brow at me, effectively calling bullshit on me. "You burn your place?"

"The night two different people tried to kill me. It's sitting there, untouched for now, but it's monitored." There was no distance to put between me and what happened, which meant I couldn't *stay* on the run. "I need a place to go. Somewhere I can stay where people won't ask questions and leave me alone."

"Fuck, Peaches. You're scared." It wasn't a statement so I didn't bother answering. "Holy shit. Even when that FBI agent threatened to put you in supermax you weren't scared. What the fuck is CAD?"

I forgot Vivi had opted out of government work after her paid servitude was up.

"Covert Affairs Division. It's one of the intelligence agencies, but it's under the DoD." That was because everyone knew the military got away with a lot more than any other agency. If there was a side to be on when shady shit went down, it was theirs.

"Damn. Defense Department shit is no joke. Have you been able to reach your contact?"

"Bob?" I snorted because that was a fucking joke. "Nope, and if I see her on the streets, I swear to God I will fuck her up so bad they'll put me on the top of every goddamn watch list in the world. Fucking Bob Slauson is the one who *accidentally* sent me the fucking video file! I know that bitch did it to get me killed. Fucking bitch." I meant every damn word and I was ready to see it through. But only if I had to.

"Told you to stay with us in Mayhem. But no, always about those dollars."

"Viv, I can't live my life like you do." I scoffed at her. "You know that."

The servers brought out more sushi and sake than two people needed. Vivi told me all about how happy she was with Jag.

"I know, and I know it sounds cheesy and stupid, but remember when we would mock happy endings because we knew it wasn't in the cards for us? Well. Jag and I are a happy ending. That's how it feels."

A smile crossed my face at her words. "I'm happy for you Vivi, really and truly. Jag seems like a good guy."

But if he ever made her regret loving him, I'd fuck him up, I said to myself.

We took a few minutes to dig into all the sushi options laid out before us, inhaling California roll bites, dragon rolls and more raw fish than anyone needed. "There is one place. No one but the Bastards knows about it, and you'd definitely be safe."

I leaned in and held my breath, waiting for her to tell me about this place that sounded too good to be true. "Can it be traced back to me?"

"Nope." Her smile was the first clue that I wouldn't like her answer but I was in a bind and we both knew it. Beggars couldn't be choosers and all that. "Gunnar has a new place down in a small Texas town."

"Fuck me sideways. My only hope is a guy who hates my fucking guts?"

"He doesn't hate you. He just doesn't trust you. His whole life is about his little sister and you…"

"Don't remind me. Fuck me if the guy can't take a joke."

Okay, so it wasn't a joke. I just didn't think it was that big of a deal to take Maisie out on a play date, but whatever. Gunnar wasn't the first man to dislike me, and he wouldn't be the last, but it had been a long time since I'd found myself at the mercy of a man with hate in his eyes.

"I'll figure something out. Don't worry, girl. I gotta get going."

"Seriously?" Vivi leaned in, fire spitting in her gray eyes. "You just told me you've got a legit hit on your life from the goddamn United States covert government shit, and then you say *don't worry about it*? Pull your fuckin' head out of your ass, Peaches. Gunnar may be grumpy but he won't turn you away. And no one will find you there."

I had my doubts about him but kept them to myself. There was a damn good chance that I'd get down to Texas, and he'd tell me to get the fuck out, but right now he was a shot. If only for a little while. "Well, if he doesn't let me stay, I keep moving. Simple as that. I'll let you know."

"You sure you can't stay any longer? I'm gonna miss you. Again."

I shook my head. "I wish I could but the fuckers with guns will be right behind me. And they know I was here last year. Get home and be safe. Tell the guys what's going on so they're on alert."

"Of course," she said with tears swimming in her eyes. "As soon as this is all over, we're doing a girls weekend."

I nodded but my heart wasn't in it. As much as I'd love to pretend things were going to be all right, I wasn't so sure. "Sure, Vivi. See you around, chica." I gave her a massive hug, nearly squishing her small frame to death as I inhaled her scent. She was my best friend, and we'd been through so much together, friends since we were teenagers. Now we were grown women with grown up problems. I would miss the hell out of her. "Take care of yourself."

"That's my line. Call every few days so I know you're alive. Otherwise, I'll see you in Texas"

I knew she meant it so I gave her a salute, paid the bill and went outside to suck in one last gulp of dry Nevada desert air. Then I got into my crappy rental, cranked up some Janis Joplin and aimed my car toward Texas.

Land of sexy grumpy men.

Chapter Five

Gunnar

"Why's Gunny cookin'?" Maisie sat in one of the oversized chairs looking adorable and ridiculous at the brand new kitchen table. Made from real pine, it was large enough to sit twenty if I added the two inserts and pushed the matching benches underneath.

"Because," I said. "Miss Martha has Saturdays off so she can rest her bones and take care of her own family. You don't like my cooking?" I gave her a fake pout that made her giggle.

"Whatcha making?"

I looked down at the stove, the spaghetti sauce bubbling in the pot. I hadn't done much to it, just added some salt and pepper but suddenly it didn't seem like enough. "Spaghetti."

"With hot dogs?"

I groaned. That shit was disgusting. "No, with spaghetti and sauce." Maybe there should be a salad? From my years taking care of Maisie, I already knew she needed fresh fruits and vegetables, but I didn't have the energy tonight. The first week at Hardtail had been long. And busy. The books were a mess, but I couldn't exactly get mad at Holden since the man wasn't an accountant or bookkeeper, but dammit, I wanted to be mad at someone.

A new contractor had finally started and promised there would be more progress soon. If not, I'd bury him somewhere on the property and hire someone else.

"But Gunny, that's gross."

"No Squirt, hot dogs and spaghetti is nasty." She huffed her disapproval but otherwise kept her mouth shut.

"Sorry to bother you Gunnar, but you have a visitor." Holden's deep voice sounded over the low hum of music and Maisie's humming when he came through the back door.

"A visitor? Impossible." None of the guys would make the trip down without calling ahead and there was no one else.

And then a new voice added, "Not impossible, exactly."

I knew that voice. Goddammit, that voice still sometimes haunted my dreams along with the killer curves that had my hands itching to wrap around any part of her. I didn't want to turn around because I didn't want it to be true. It couldn't be true. But it had to be true. That voice belonged to no one else on this earth.

Slowly I turned, steeling myself for what I would see. "Peaches." Her name came out as a groan, which I hadn't intended, but dammit the woman was a menace. "What are you doing here?"

She froze, big brown eyes wary and tired but not just tired. No, she looked scared too. "I was hoping you had a spare bed for a while?" She looked back and forth between me and Holden, clearly hesitant to say anymore in front of someone she didn't know.

"No, I don't." Yeah, I was an asshole, and I knew it, but everything about Peaches screamed trouble, and I had no use for trouble in my life these days. Especially someone who could put Maisie's life in danger.

She looked at me, her face free of makeup for once, which made her look young, almost innocent. She'd hidden her wild curls under a baseball cap and even her curves were disguised behind a khaki skirt and pink tank top. "Not even for a night or two? Please, Gunnar?"

The tension in her voice should have softened me, but it only made me harden more. "Why?"

She glanced at Holden again and then back to me, before she realized Maisie was sitting there. "Hey Maze, lookin' good kiddo."

"Peaches, it's you!" Maisie scrambled off the chair and took a running start at the curvy vixen, flying into her waiting arms. "I missed you, Peaches!"

"I missed you too kid. So much," my nemesis said and closed her eyes as she hugged my sister tight. "In fact," she looked up at me again, her expression blank, "I was just passing through, and figured I should come say hello to my favorite little girl."

"Really?"

"Yep. Glad to see you're taking to the cowgirl life, kiddo."

Maisie giggled and put both of her little hands on Peaches' cheeks. "It's so pretty here, Peaches."

"Pretty place for a pretty little girl. Anyway," she said and set my sister on her feet before taking a step back. "I just stopped in to say hey to you but now I need to get going." Her voice wobbled, and it damn near got me when she swallowed again, trying to hide the emotion in her voice.

"You can't stay for dinner?" How she was able to resist Maisie's face, I'd never know.

"Sorry, but I've got a drive ahead of me, Maze. Maybe next time, okay?"

"No! Peaches. Stay!"

"I can't honey. Bye sweet girl." She gave me one last, emotionless look and walked right back through the open front door.

Holden questioned me with his eyes, but I just shook my head. "Thanks."

"You sure? If you need to talk to her, I'll look after the little one."

I appreciated the offer, but I wanted no part of whatever trouble she'd gotten herself into. "No thanks. Want to stay for dinner, Holden?"

"Got a date. Ran into your friend on the road. She had missed the turn, so I brought her here."

A date? I hadn't been on a date in too damn long and worse, I didn't even miss it. Barely thought of it except for those few weeks Peaches spent at the clubhouse. Helping us out.

"Dammit." I said to Holden. "Give me a sec?"

Holden didn't even try to hide his smile as he winked down at Maisie. "Don't you think Peaches is pretty, Holden?"

I sped up because I didn't want to hear the answer to that. If I was lucky, Peaches would already be gone leaving nothing but a dust trail in her wake, but I'd never had much luck. Or much sense either because I kept moving toward the driver's side door, determined to tell her she couldn't stay here. As I got closer, I realized her shoulders were hunched over the steering wheel and she'd buried her face in her arms. Crying. Fuck. No man could stand to see a woman cry, and I was no exception. Tapping on the window, I expected a scream of surprise or something.

Not a blank look when she spotted me. In true smartass Peaches style, she rolled her window down about three inches. "Yes?"

"What kind of trouble are you in?"

"I'm not in any kind of trouble, and I'll be out of here in a minute." With those words, she rolled the window back up and her head went back down.

I tapped on the window again and this time she glared. "Why did you come here?" I hadn't made my feelings about her a secret so she must be in bad shape to ask for my help. And I was an ass to her.

"I didn't." She turned the key until the engine started and shifted gears. "I'm not here. In fact, I was never here."

"Peaches, dammit. Can you be serious for one minute?"

"I shouldn't have come here, that's obvious. Vivi thought you might be able to help me out, but I knew you wouldn't, so the rest doesn't matter. Have a nice life, Gunnar."

This was the thanks men got when they tried to help out a stubborn ass woman. "You can stay."

"It's not nec—"

"—Stay in the goddamn bunkhouse. And you leave when I say go." I wondered if she would throw the offer back in my face and speed off anyway, but after a few really long minutes, she killed the engine.

"I just need to get a plan in place and then I'm gone." I didn't say anything to that because, honestly, I didn't believe her. "I came to you because there's no connection to me, Gunnar. No other reason."

"Good, because Maisie—"

She cut me off. "Is great and I would die before I let anything happen to her. A few days and then I'm gone, I swear."

If she were any other woman, I might not have believed her, but I caught a glimpse of what it cost her to ask for help. So I just nodded and walked to the porch. "If you're staying, you might as well come for dinner."

"Only if you're sure," she called back.

"I'm not sure of a goddamn thing except that I'm hungry. Now come eat, or don't." After dinner tonight, I'd keep my distance. With Peaches in the bunkhouse and me getting the club off the ground, we'd hardly see each other.

Chapter Six

Peaches

The bunkhouse. Gunnar had put me in the bunkhouse. Though I was grateful, I also kind of resented the hell out of him for being so damn gruff and angry, and then putting me in a bare bones square structure that looked more like a prison than a home.

I stepped inside the squat wooden building, letting the screen door smack shut behind me and froze. Okay, so maybe it was more like a dorm room, a boy's dorm with jeans and boxers tossed over every single bed with no distinction between clean and dirty clothes. A few smartphones charged on a table in the corner, the low hum of country music played from another part of the building, but otherwise the place appeared to be empty.

"Home sweet home." At least for a few days. It was clear Gunnar didn't want me around and the truth was, I didn't blame him. The guy was a world-class jerk if I'd ever met one, but his kid sister's safety was his top priority. I knew my being here screwed with that. So a few days to get a strategy in place, and then I'd be back on the road, headed...somewhere.

Anywhere.

A door opened to my left and a man strolled out. A naked man with smooth tan skin, tattoos and muscles everywhere. Everywhere. His chest was big and wide, pecs large and topped with light brown nipples. He looked to have some Hispanic in him, but those blue eyes and that blondish brown hair gave him a wildly exotic look that was enough to make me stare like a schoolgirl. A horny schoolgirl.

"Well, hello there roomie," I said. I winked at the delicious specimen and his cheeks turned the cutest shade of pink. "I'm Peaches."

"Peaches." He said my name like it was a word he wasn't used to, testing it on his tongue before he turned to me with a sheepish smile. "Peaches the roomie, eh?" Oh he was more comfortable now, with me and his nudity which was fine with me because well, he was damn fine.

"Gunnar's letting me crash in here for a few days." I took a step back to let the man get a towel or some clothes, both of which would be a travesty, but blocking him further would make me a creep.

"And your name is Peaches?" I nodded, waiting for all the jokes men came up with that they all thought were just so fucking hilarious. "I'm Cruz. Nice to meet you." He held his hand out and gave me a firm shake which I appreciated. Some men gave a weak-wristed version of a handshake that was more than a little insulting.

"You, too, and I'd love to apologize for the ogling, but I meant to do it, so sorry if it made you uncomfortable."

"Once I realized you weren't crazy, I was kind of flattered," he admitted with a flush of pink infusing his cheeks.

"Good. Because that would have made the next few days a little awkward."

Cruz flashed another gorgeous grin and stepped into a pair of plain gray boxer briefs that made me turn away like a prude. "Take any bed you'd like. This one and that one are being used now. That might change in a few days though."

This room held five bunks, none of which were actual bunk beds, thank goodness. I chose the one with the least amount of crap on it and dropped my bags right on top. There was no bedding, which made me happy for the shopping trip I'd made a couple hours before I made it to The Hardtail Ranch.

In anticipation of Gunnar's rejection, I'd stocked up on camping supplies while passing through Dallas. The best way to stay off the grid was to go all the way off the grid, an unappealing plan that I still couldn't dismiss outright.

"Thanks. What do you do around here, Cruz?" I hadn't taken much time to look around, but I'd done a quick search on the place before I arrived. I knew it was a working ranch. "You look like a cowboy but everything about you screams military."

"Even the beard?" He stroked the sculpted honey blond hair on his face with a smile.

"Especially the beard. The first signs of someone fresh from the military is either facial hair or long hair. The beard does not scream cowboy though."

His smile was somehow boyish but also gorgeous. "That's 'cause I'm not a cowboy. Not yet anyway."

"Other than a vet, what are you?"

Cruz shrugged. "Trying to figure that part out. All the guys here so far are vets. My superior officer knows Gunnar and said he'd told him Hardtail Ranch was a place a vet could go to figure his shit out. So here I am."

"That sounds… oddly nice for the perpetual asshole named Gunner that I know." It was completely out of character for him, then again, I'd seen him be nice and sweet to Maisie, his motorcycle club, and even Vivi and Moon. Maybe it was just me who brought out the asshole in him. Wouldn't be the first time. "Nice."

Cruz's deep chuckle bounced around the empty walls and open windows. "You're safe, darlin'."

Realizing he must've taken my tone as something else, I rushed to correct him. "I'm not worried about my safety Cruz. The guy you described sounds nothing like the Gunnar I know is all."

"Then I hope you get to meet the guy I know." His words were sincere, and I knew that despite whatever problems he had, Cruz seemed like one of the good ones. There weren't many of 'em out there, which made it easy to spot them when you found one.

"I'm glad you have a soft place to land Cruz, but I won't be here long enough for that. In fact, I better get to it."

He nodded his understanding but there was a hint of something in his eyes I refused to think too long about. He had his opinion of Gunnar, and I had mine. End of story.

"The chow hall is on the other side of this wall. Miss Martha does breakfast and supper for the ranch hands at seven and four."

"Thanks Cruz." I turned to give the man enough privacy that he could finish dressing and when I turned back, he was gone, which made it the perfect time to grab a shower. Unlike my roomie, I brought my clothes into the bathroom with me. In fact, all of my belongings came into the bathroom with me.

What could I say? I had trust issues.

***

Three days of Gunnar's attempt at hospitality and I still didn't know what the hell I was going to do. There were plenty of plans jotted down but none of them were long-term options. Some required more time to plan than I had and others were more suited to someone hiding out from local cops, not the U.S. government and certainly not hired assassins. Which meant that in seventy-two hours I'd accomplished absolutely nothing.

The Texas heat was hot as hell, and I only had a few changes of clothes. Rather than risk the burning sun, I stayed inside on my bunk hunched over my laptop. None of the guys seemed bothered by my appearance, mostly ignoring me other than to let me know when meal time rolled around. Cruz seemed to want to look after me while the other guy, Joplin was content to pretend I was invisible.

That was fine by me. The last thing I needed was another grumpy ass man to deal with. Not that I'd had any grumpy men to deal with lately because Gunnar and I had done a spectacular job of ignoring each other. He didn't need to come to the bunkhouse for any reason so he didn't. The fewer run-ins with him, the better.

I'd just connected to the video feed in my old apartment when the front door of the bunkhouse smacked open and another tall, gorgeous man with wide shoulders stepped inside. His face was unfamiliar and the duffel bag in his hand pegged him as a new arrival. Clear blue eyes connected with mine in a dark frown, and the man took a step back like a jumpy cat. "Hey."

His frown only darkened. "Who are you?"

I ignored his surly behavior but dropped the smile. "Does it matter? I'll be gone before you learn my name. There are five additional bunks on the other side of the chow hall if you're uncomfortable here." Because he most certainly was, discomfort was written all over him.

"Thanks," he bit out and turned on his heels, giving me his fine backside as he stomped away to the other side of the bunkhouse.

I shrugged, unfazed by his unfriendly behavior and went back to the footage of my apartment. No one had entered in the first twenty-four hours or the next twenty-four, which had given me a false sense of relief because at the tail end of day three, a man dressed in black appeared.

He was covered from head to toe in black clothing and coverings, so even his race was concealed thanks to the balaclava he wore. I watched carefully as he went through every inch of my apartment in search of that footage probably, or my whereabouts. To his credit, the man searched meticulously and all without leaving any traces that he'd been there, going through what he assumed were my personal belongings.

I'd left nothing there for him to find, of course, but that only meant they weren't done hunting for me. Which meant I needed a better plan. Fast.

The door slammed open again and a Jason Momoa look-alike stepped inside. Tall, dark and bearded with a charming smile that didn't quite reach his eyes, the man didn't bother looking my way as he set his bag on the bed right beside me. Finally his coffee-colored gaze landed on me. "Didn't know there were chicks here too."

I arched a brow at his comment. "No chicks in your branch of the service?"

"Who said I was military?"

Only everything so I rolled my eyes at his non-denial denial. "I'm not here and I won't be for much longer. You and your belongings are safe from my girl cooties."

Finally, the tall gorgeous man looked at me and burst out laughing. It was a good sound, rich and deep and full of life. "I'm Slayer."

"Great name, I'm Peaches. I can just guess how you got that nickname." As his brows arched, I laughed too. "Unless you're from the only town in the world with actual dragons, it's not too hard a guess."

Slayer laughed again and ripped off his black t-shirt to reveal a mouthwatering six pack and thick biceps that were perfect for a woman to hold on to. Just as quickly he replaced it with another black t-shirt and looked around the empty bunkhouse. Warily.

I let out a sigh and sank further against the wall. "There's another five beds on the other side of the chow hall."

"Nah, I prefer to go to bed and wake up with a view. Even if it's one I can't touch."

My lips curled into a smile. "Smart man. Too bad I've got my own problems. Adding you to the list isn't in the cards." But damn! I really could use a hard male body to satisfy my needs and distract me for a few hours.

"But it'd be fun," he said with a smile, and I had no doubt Slayer was a man who could deliver on that promise.

"Without a doubt. If I live through the next bit of my life, I'll give it some serious thought." He frowned at my words, but before he could ask about my cryptic comment, another flash of movement drew my eyes back to my screen. It wasn't the same man; this one was bigger and he didn't do nearly as good a job at hiding his identity. I grabbed a screenshot of his image and attached it to an email from my fictional personal assistant to the NYPD.

"Good luck, then."

"Thanks, Slayer. Welcome to Hardtail Ranch."

He stopped in the doorway. Outlined by the midday sun, he looked every inch the sexy rake he appeared to be. "Thanks, Peaches."

Left with my own thoughts I realized why the men had come back to my old apartment. They lost my trail and were trying to find a loose thread, which would have made this a perfect time to execute a plan. If I fucking had one.

A good plan. A doable plan. One that wouldn't end up with me caught or dead in six months. I could disappear to Mexico and change my identity before heading to Europe. I could hitch a ride on a boat to Australia, getting rid of all traces of my old self. Or…

It was that fucking *or* that kept me up most nights. I couldn't leave without knowing what and where, but I couldn't stay much longer. Every day I stayed here put Maisie closer to danger.

So I had to give myself an end date. A date that, no matter what happened, I would get out of here.

And never look back.

Chapter Seven

Gunnar

The only goddamn thing that seemed to be working out for me this week was that I hadn't laid eyes on Peaches since she walked in and asked to invade my space for a while. Thank God for small fucking favors since nothing else was going my way. Nothing at all. "What the hell do you mean the liquor license was denied? Fuck, this cannot be happening, Saint!" A liquor license was crucial to the running of The Barn Door.

Saints hand shook as his fingers speared through his hair and his green eyes held a hint of wariness. "I mean The Barn Door's application for a liquor license was denied. The provider who filled out the application didn't answer some questions and they kicked it back. At least that's what the letter in your hand says."

The kid wasn't as big a pussy as he seemed, which was comforting, but it didn't help my liquor license problem right now.

"What fucking provider?" I knew I should have come down sooner, but I'd been putting it off because I didn't want to have to deal with it.

Saint sighed and rolled his eyes in frustration. "That's how things are done down here, man. We have to get a *professional* to fill out the forms, but that asshole was the reason it was denied in the first damn place!"

"Goddammit! What the hell don't these fuckers understand about having booze at an adult establishment? Alcohol lowers people's inhibitions and makes them more likely to enjoy themselves, which is The Barn Door's goddamn specialty. The more booze people drink, the more money goes into the cash register. Who do I have to fuckin' talk to?"

"Albert Stinson, that rat-faced motherfucker. Charged an arm and a goddamn leg in fees, then we get rejected." Saint did some weird shit, tapping his phone to mine and then he stepped back. "That's his contact info."

"That easy? Thanks man."

"No problem, Boss. The walls and floors should be done by the end of the week."

"That's good news," I called back to him before I left the unfinished structure and whipped out my phone. The first few times I tried to get through to this asshole Stinson, the call dropped because we were out in the damn country, but as I got closer to the main house, white and gleaming in the midday sun, the call connected and stayed that way.

"Albert Stinson, how can I help you?"

"You can tell me what the fuck you did to get my liquor license rejected?" He stammered and stuttered and tried to explain but I was in no fucking mood to listen. "I don't give a shit about your excuses, Stinson. You were paid because you guaran-fucking-teed that you knew what you were doing to *ensure a smooth and painless process*. Well right now it's not smooth—or painless."

"Y-yessir. I'm looking into it, and I'll fix it. Right away."

"See that you do." I wouldn't stand for this good old boy bullshit, not when it came to my home or my business. The call ended, and I made my way across the field that would take me back to the main house, enjoying the feel of the sun beating down on my back. It was nice outside, then again it was always nice here. It was the only good thing about this fucking place so far.

It was all right; it just wasn't home.

I heard the music, loud modern country, before I saw them. Peaches and Maisie playing next to the stables in their bathing suits. A barely there bikini for the big girl and a white two-piece covered in sunflowers for the little one. Maisie's giggles sounded over the music and it pulled my lips into a big smile. It had been far too long since I heard such pure, unadulterated joy from her.

But the closer I got, the more disturbed I felt, and it had nothing to do with my sister's beautiful laugh and everything to do with the scraps of cloth Peaches called a fucking bathing suit. She had too many curves, nice round tits that were more than a handful for a big man like me. Her ass was nice and round with just a hint of a jiggle and her hips brought images to mind of my hands on her hips while I thrust deep inside her.

"Enough!"

My voice carried and two sets of eyes turned to me while some woman belted out that the next time her man cheated, it wouldn't be on her.

"Hey Gunny! We washin' cars!" Maisie waved from her perch in Peaches' arms while she scrubbed the windshield of Peaches road-worn Caddie.

"I see that." Her smile was so wide and her little girl sunglasses, that I didn't even know she had. She looked so adorable it melted my heart. Even the sunscreen streaked down her nose and across her forehead went a long way to cooling my anger. "You're getting some sun."

"I got on screen, Gunny. And water," she added and looked up at Peaches for confirmation.

"Good, but I think it's time you went inside for a while." As expected, her little shoulders fell and a pout formed on her lips.

"But we ain't done yet."

I didn't want to fight with her, but this wasn't an argument I was willing to have and certainly not here. "Peaches can finish without you."

Maisie took her sunglasses off and looked up to Peaches who just shrugged. "When parents speak, kids gotta listen, kiddo."

"Will you come and see me again, Peaches?" The moment those blue eyes slammed into hers, I could see Peaches was a goner.

"I'll try my best, Maze. Make sure you have a tall glass of water when you get inside."

Maisie scrambled out of Peaches' arms and ran across the grass as fast as her little legs would carry her.

When the door slammed behind her, Peaches turned to me, those burgundy brows arched in question. "Well?"

"What?" I didn't mean to bark at her, but goddammit, why did she have to sound so smug?

"Go ahead," she said, smug as fuck, "and say whatever the hell it is that has your fucking feathers all ruffled. You think I'm going to drown her or something this time? I know you think she isn't safe around me."

She stood there with her arms crossed in a way that drew attention to the smooth swells of honey brown skin which only made her waist look trimmer and narrower. With one hip kicked out to the side in that sassy way of hers, she looked tempting as fuck.

"My feathers ruffled? I don't get ruffled, sweetheart."

"Maybe you ought to tell your face that because you look like you sucked on a fucking lemon." Then, like I wasn't even there, she turned the hose back on and started rinsing the soap off the windshield while she sang off-key with the scorned woman on the stereo.

Chapter Eight

Peaches

He was still there. Behind me. Watching me. I could feel Gunnar's deep blue gaze staring a hole in my back. Well, my ass would be more accurate because the heat and weight of his gaze was centered right there. Either way I could feel him staring at me, but I was determined to wait him out, crusty bastard.

"Maybe I look that way because you're traipsing around naked in front of my kid sister!"

Ah, I knew it was coming. I felt his gaze on me even before Gunnar had made his presence known. There was something about him, that undefinable quality that made his gaze, his mere presence a palpable *thing*.

"Naked?" I whirled around and glared at him as I stepped from the fender of my Cadillac. "I'm wearing a fucking bathing suit, Gunnar. A bikini! Don't blame me that your hormones can't handle it."

Because that was exactly what this was. He'd gotten a boner in his sister's presence and it humiliated him or whatever other irrational emotion men succumbed to but pretended they didn't.

"You couldn't have worn a fucking t-shirt?" He stepped forward, getting close enough to *try* to intimidate me, but I'd seen at least a thousand men like Gunnar in my life and none of them scared me. None at all.

"Why should I when it's hot as balls out here and it's not like she hasn't seen it all before."

Spending time with Vivi, Moon, Teddy, Jana and Mandy meant the little girl was well versed in all things female.

He pulled himself up to his full height. "You don't live here alone, Peaches. There are men here who might think wearing this is an offer of sorts."

I sucked in a breath, offended that he would even say such a thing about the men he'd invited to live on his ranch. "So what you're saying is that you brought a bunch of degenerates to live on your ranch with your sister? Good to know. I'll sleep with one eye open."

He opened his mouth and closed it and yeah, maybe I stared a little too long at those soft pink lips, but I could hate him and still think he was hot as shit.

"I didn't say that."

"No but you implied it. I'll be sure to let them know what you think of them."

I would do no such thing, of course, but Gunnar needed to be taken down a peg or two. "As always, it was good talking to you Gunnar."

"We're not done talking yet." His voice was loud and his tone was firm and cold. Angry. "Don't walk away from me."

"Don't think of it as walking away from you, Gunny. Think of it as me walking to my *bunk*house. Where I *bunk* with the degenerates."

I laughed at the rumbling growl that sounded behind me. I'd pissed Gunnar off and nothing was more fun than when the man couldn't keep his emotions under control.

"We'll finish this later, Peaches."

"No, we won't."

I was pretty sure I heard him mumble, "Stubborn damn woman," under his breath as he stalked away. I walked over to the bunkhouse with a big, shit eating grin on my face.

Chapter Nine

Gunnar

Goddamn infuriating woman. That was what she was, infuriating. First, running around Hardtail Ranch without any clothes on and then accusing me of being pissed off because I liked what I saw. Goddamn right I liked what I saw! I was a red-blooded man who couldn't get enough of a beautiful, curvy woman. Especially a lively one like her. But it could never be anything else. Just pure sexual release, and she would be out of my fucking head for good.

It was too damn bad I didn't know a single fuckable woman in the entire state of Texas other than the one I mostly definitely would not be shoving my cock into tonight.

"Dammit!" The woman was in my head and it was not where I needed her to be. Anywhere else but there. She was too dangerous to be around Maisie. Too much covert work and undercover secrets and undesirables around her. And that was reason enough for me to want her out of here. I'd upended my whole life for Maisie, and I wasn't going to have some CIA or NSA or secret government chick screw things up, I didn't care how gorgeous her tits were.

A quick ice cold shower was the first thing I did when I entered the house. Sounds of Maisie and Martha's laughter filtered from the kitchen, but I didn't want to hear them, not now. Not when my mind was full of a honey-skinned temptress with the body of a goddess. The cold water was refreshing, but it didn't do a damn thing to quell the fire in my belly for Peaches so there was only one thing to do.

I grabbed my cock in my hand and stroked it while I thought of her soft hands in place of mine. Her husky voice saying dirty shit to me while she tugged on my cock, bringing me closer and closer to the edge. I closed my eyes and braced a hand on the wall while the icy water rushed over me, jerking my cock to the image of Peaches down on her knees, plump lips open wide to take my dick between those luscious lips.

"Oh fuck!" My jizz went everywhere, releasing the tension in my body with every spurt of the hot white stuff.

My breaths were shallow as the orgasm spilled out of my body, and I turned the water to hot, giving myself a few minutes to think about what I'd just done. Jerked off to the vision of a woman I couldn't fucking stand. But wanted desperately. Even that, as brief and satisfying as it had been, wasn't enough to keep the woman from invading my thoughts.

After finding another pair of jeans and a clean t-shirt that was in the wrong damn spot, courtesy of the useless Bennett twins, I made my way down to the kitchen. The kitchen crowded with all the hands and staff and our guest Peaches, sitting around a table groaning with a feast. "Did my invite get lost in the mail?"

Martha whirled away from the stove with a contagious smile on her face. "Just in time, Gunnar. I thought it would be nice to welcome all the new faces to Hardtail Ranch with a proper ranch supper."

It was a proper supper all right. Martha had piled the table high with barbecue brisket and fried chicken, mac & cheese, collard greens, mashed potatoes and gravy, plus a big basket of rolls.

The kitchen was quiet, breath held as they waited for my reaction. Most of them wore hesitant expressions, wondering if I would act a fool or accept the dinner as it was. Evelyn and Adrian looked bored but I did catch them peeking at all the new faces around the table. Peaches though, wore a smug grin like she knew that this was the last damn thing I wanted on a Friday night, especially after the fucking week I had.

"I'd say you put out a hell of a spread, Miss Martha. I hope you plan on joining us?"

Her cheeks turned pink and her hand went to her large bosom. "Well if you insist, Gunnar. I have a special treat once dinner is done. Eat up, boys and girls."

I took one of the two seats left available and it happened to be right beside the woman I'd just jerked off to. At least she had on more clothes than she'd been wearing earlier, though not much more. The straps of her sundress were so damn tiny that a gust of wind could unravel them and reveal her tits to the whole table, but the swells of her cleavage were the real rock stars, high and brown with just enough jiggle every time she moved. Or laughed and Peaches laughed a lot.

"Miss Martha, this is the best brisket I've ever had and one of my foster moms made a divine brisket." Peaches flashed a bright smile Martha's way and the older woman ate it up, flushing at the compliment. "You'll fatten these boys right up."

Martha laughed. "That's music to my ears, honey. These boys are fine men, but some of them could use a bit more meat on their bones."

"I don't know, Mama, I think they're all pretty meaty," Evelyn said, leaning toward Cruz who leaned away from her. "Who woulda thought so many fine men would come to our little ol' town and fall right in our laps?"

Peaches snickered and Maisie joined in because my sister, for some reason, thought she hung the moon.

"They are," Peaches agreed. "And thank you all for your service." She flashed that damn smile again, at each of the men at the table. Including me.

Slayer winked. "You're welcome, honey," he said, which only made her laugh.

The rest of the boys joined in with less flirtatious words of thanks and her grin widened.

"Thank you," Maisie parroted back, earning a few laughs and plenty of smiles.

Dinner passed in a blur of food and iced tea, soda and the best part of all was Miss Martha's surprise. Peach cobbler and cherry pie.

"Hot damn, Miss Martha, will you adopt me?" Peaches said. She made loud erotic noises with every bite. I wasn't the only one who'd noticed, though most of the other guys seemed amused by her, more than aroused.

"You flatter an old woman," she insisted with a dismissive wave but Peaches was not deterred.

"Trust me I've blown smoke plenty but this pie is a religious experience. You could sell these at twenty-five bucks a pop. I'd buy one until my ass started to protest."

She smiled again and happily took another slice, oblivious to the nasty looks the Bennett twins sent her way.

"Thank you, Peaches," Martha said. "You're such a sweet girl."

She smiled again but this time it was more genuine and less sassy, less phony than her others. "Thank you, Miss Martha."

I leaned back from the table, my buttons starting to pop. "Thank you for a delicious meal Miss Martha." It was damn good and my stomach was close to bursting.

The kitchen cleared out soon after the last slice of pie had been eaten, with the twins following the ranch hands out to the bunkhouse or wherever they planned to spend the night. Martha got up from the table and began gathering plates, but Peaches placed a hand on her shoulder. "One thing foster care taught me, Miss Martha, is that the cook doesn't wash the dishes. So you go on home. I'll take care of it." She kissed the woman on the cheek, drawing another damn blush and earning her a big motherly hug.

"Thank you, honey. Have a good night."

"Will do. You too." Martha laughed and gathered her things before shuffling out quietly.

I sat at the table and watched Peaches move easily around the kitchen, grabbing plates and cups to rinse before putting them in the dishwasher. She hummed to herself as she worked, completely fucking ignoring me. "I guess you expect me to help?"

"I'll help," Maisie offered with an excited wave of her arms.

Peaches turned around and smiled at Maisie. "Thanks for the offer, but it's almost your bedtime little girl. All this food has made you sleepy."

"I'm not," she insisted even as her lids began to droop and her head started to bob in all directions. "I'm...not."

Peaches just laughed and turned back to the sink, washing and rinsing and stacking until all that was left were the pots and pans. And all I could do was watch. And fantasize about her naked, wet and moaning around my cock. "I'll go put her to bed."

She didn't say one fucking word as I lifted my sister in my arms and left the kitchen.

Infuriating damn woman.

***

By the time I got Maisie to bed and read her two stories, at least thirty minutes had gone by. The kitchen was empty along with the rest of the house, because I looked. There was no fucking trace of Peaches, and I couldn't decide if I was pissed off, disappointed or happy as hell to have that temptation as far the fuck away from me as possible on this ranch.

I grabbed a beer and made my way to my favorite spot on Hardtail Ranch, the front porch. This time of night the moon hung fat and low in the sky, almost like it was shining just to light up the land just for me. The bunkhouse was spotlighted like the perfect scene right out of a western movie and goddammit, this place was growing on me. It wasn't quite home yet, but it was starting to become home-*like*.

A movement in the field to the right caught my eye. Two long shapely legs shot right up in the air and then back down before crossing at the knees.

"Fucking Peaches." Before I could think better of it, me and my beer were headed right for her moonlit silhouette. "What are you doing now?"

She was laid out on a flannel blanket, her dress replaced with a pair of short denim shorts and a sleeveless white shirt but all I could see was the stiff peaks of her nipples. "It seems like I'm plotting to fuck up your life, but really I'm just enjoying being able to see the stars at night."

Damn woman. Laid out like that, she looked like a fucking snack and I wanted to dive right in. "Can't you ever just answer a fucking question?"

"Ask a real question and I might surprise you." Her words were filled with amusement, but her expression was blank and her eyes never left the twinkling lights in the sky.

"Why are you laying out here in the grass?"

She shrugged. "I've always lived in the city so this is a nice view. I figured I might as well take advantage of it while I'm here."

"Which will be for how much longer?"

Finally she looked up at me, her big brown eyes so damn bottomless they looked black in the moonlight. But they gave nothing away, no hint of what she was feeling. Peaches sat up, leaning back on her elbows as if she knew how great it made her tits look. "When do you want me gone, Gunnar?"

I sighed. That was a hard damn question to answer. The truth was that I wanted her gone yesterday, but I couldn't very well say that.

"Right." She was up on her feet in one quick as lightning ninja move that would have impressed me if she hadn't used that time to walk away from me. Again.

"Peaches. Stop."

"No thanks, Gunnar. I'm not interested in anymore of your illuminating conversation."

She could try to run, but I had six inches on her. Plus, I was faster. "I'm not asking." It was an ill-advised move to put a hand on an angry woman, but I was too focused on getting her to stop to realize that. "Dammit, woman."

"Get your fucking hands off of me." Her voice was cool and restrained, no hint of panic or any sign she was in distress. It was fucking impressive. "I won't ask again."

"You didn't ask this time." Damn she was fiery as fuck and up close like this, with that sexy scent wafting from her slightly overheated skin, I couldn't deny how much I wanted her.

"When you put your hands on me without my permission, I don't ask. Let me go." She tried to pull her arm away but my grip was strong. Firm. "Gunnar."

"Make me." A smarter man might have taken a moment to think about his actions, but no one had ever accused me of being smart.

"Don't be an asshole." Still, she didn't show any anger. Her words were cursory, almost like she'd checked out, but I knew that wasn't the case. Her fist went up, and I knew it was headed right to my left cheek.

I was too fast. "I wouldn't advise that."

"The next target will be your nuts if you don't get your fucking hands off me." I held onto her for a few seconds longer, eager to see what she would do. Her knee came up, and I twisted to the side, giving her the opportunity to break free.

"Damn you, Peaches. Why are you so fucking annoying?"

"You know what? Fuck you, Gunnar. Fuck off!" She whirled around, and I knew once she was inside the bunkhouse, whatever was happening between us would be over.

"Stop." I spun her back to me until we were chest to chest. Hers was soft and smooth, pillowy against my hard muscles. She looked up at me surprised, shocked even, but I could see desire swimming in her eyes. Peaches wanted me as much as I wanted her.

It was decided then, by powers greater than me, and my mouth crashed down on hers. Soft lips touched my own, hesitant at first because we kind of hated each other. Or at least thought we did. She submitted to me, leaning against my chest while she gripped my shoulders and I devoured her mouth. And Lord have mercy, she tasted of cherries and whatever sweet shit she slicked on her lips.

I needed more. More of her sweet, warm mouth and more of those lush curves pressed right where I needed them. Using my body I pushed her up against the nearest hard surface, an old oak tree. When Peaches moaned in my mouth, I lost it. My hands went everywhere, gripping her delicious fucking hips and squeezing her ass, thinking about doing the same thing while I fucked her from behind. But when my hands reached her sweet, bouncy tits, I was lost.

"Fuck!" I grabbed the collar of her shirt and ripped it down the center until her beautiful tits were bared. Just for me. Her skin was honey brown with big, caramel colored nipples that made my mouth water. "You make me crazy."

"Join the club," she panted and speared her fingers through my hair as I leaned in for a quick taste. "Yes! Fuck, yes!" She pulled me closer and I took advantage, kissing and licking and sucking hard tipped nipples until she started to grind against me.

Back and forth, I loved on her beautiful tits until her hand found my cock, hard and aching. "Peaches."

"Yeah?" She kept stroking through my jeans, driving me out of my goddamn mind with her sexy little moans and her throaty cries. "Somebody's ready to play," she cooed playfully.

I growled and shoved my fingers in her shorts, smiling wide at the feel of all that wet pussy waiting for me. "Looks like I'm not the only one," I told her as one finger slipped inside. She was hot and wet. Judging by the way her pussy clamped around my finger, she was also close.

So fucking close.

"Gunnar, stop teasing." Before I could say another word, my cock was free and her soft warm hand stroked me back and forth. Back and forth. Her thumb slicked over the pre-come and rubbed it all around my cock until I groaned.

"Now who's teasing?" I lifted her in my arms, smiling at the delightful squeal she let out when her back hit the tree trunk. "Last chance to back out."

She smiled wickedly and licked her lips. "Shut up and fuck me."

She shimmied out of her shorts and bared her sweet, commando pussy.

I wasn't gonna argue with that because I could feel her arousal, so potent my cock leaked over her fist. "Since you asked so nicely."

"Fuck, yes." The words came out on a hiss as my cock went deep inside her wet pussy, getting acquainted with all her soft lusciousness. "Gunnar, yes!" Peaches was wild, pulling on my hair and scraping her teeth up and down my neck as she ground against my cock. She took her pleasure, using my cock like a fuck toy, and I wouldn't have it any other way.

"Slow down, girl. We have all night." Or at least I hoped we did.

"No. Can't." She breathed out.

Her fingers dug into my shoulders, holding on tight while she fucked me. Hard and fast, her hips rolled while I pumped into her with wild abandon, losing myself in the feel of her. The way her cunt felt clenching around my cock as she came undone, her juices covered my cock, increasing the friction until it was like fucking in zero gravity.

"Gunnar," she crooned. Deep brown eyes held mine captive, looking into them like she could see my every fucking secret, but that wasn't what Peaches was looking for.

She held my gaze as the orgasm worked its way up her body until it erupted, explosive and vibrant. She vibrated as the waves of pleasure shot out of her, still bouncing on my cock while I slammed into her.

And then she was spent.

Limp in my arms.

I smiled. Now that I'd had her, I could get back to the shit that really mattered.

Chapter Ten

Peaches

Lying under the tree with Gunnar as moonlight filtered down on our naked bodies, I felt relaxed. No, not relaxed, sated. My body was no longer tense, my muscles had lost the knotted lumps that kept me on edge twenty four seven for the past few weeks. That was what a really good orgasm did for a girl, left her dickmatized so she'd forget all her problems and worries.

At least temporarily.

That was the problem with dick, the high never lasted long, not even when it was damn good dick. Like Gunnar's. The man was long and thick which was always nice, but what was even better, he knew how to use it, fucking me hard and deep until I couldn't think straight. And the dick-high lasted a record forty-five minutes, for which I was grateful. But the moment it was gone, the fear and anger, the paranoia, anxiety and even the nausea returned.

With wicked fucking abandon.

As good as the weight of Gunnar's overheated arm felt across my waist, I had to get away. From his overwhelming scent and the masculinity of him, to the way it felt to be in his arms. Not his arms exactly, just a man's arms. It was nice and warm and safe, and that was a fucking lie. There was nothing safe—or nice—about him and it was that thought that pulled me out of his arms and onto the dewy grass. Digging my knees into the grass, I stood and tied a knot in my shirt, then pulled on my shorts so I could walk to the bunkhouse with some dignity.

Not that there was much dignity in letting a guy who hated me fuck me up against a tree, then again dignity wasn't what I was after with him.

Still, I stood tall and made my way to the bunkhouse, thankful it was too early for any of the guys to be back from a night of trouble making. Taking advantage of the alone time, I grabbed the necessities and took a quick shower to get rid of the smell of sex—and Gunnar.

I knew sleep wouldn't come easy so I didn't bother trying, opening my laptop instead to check on the state of things back in New York. There'd been no more movement inside my apartment other than a few dozen menus shoved under the door.

But I got hit with a news alert about my second-floor studio that made me sick. *"Transient, Wallace Roosevelt Carver, was found dead in an unoccupied second floor apartment. Authorities believe the cause of death was heat exposure."* The article went on to talk about the homeless problem in the city as the temperatures hit record highs and some other bullshit about the risks of exposure. I knew it wasn't the heat, but some cold blooded asshole who didn't care about human life at all.

My heart broke for Wallace. He was a good man who'd fallen on hard times and got used to living a hard life. He was harmless and wouldn't hurt anyone. The man didn't know anything useful or real about me, either. Dammit!

Just one thought came on the heels of my guilt and sadness over Wallace. *Maisie.* I couldn't risk her safety, and I wouldn't put her in danger just to save myself. As I thought about it, I wouldn't put any of the guys at risk. They were honorable men who'd fought hard for people who didn't deserve it and had become broken for their efforts. I couldn't interfere with the healing that was going on at the Hardtail Ranch.

I wouldn't.

I had to leave. My problem was I had nowhere to go. I jumped off the bed and shut my laptop, scanning the room for anything that belonged to me. It was best to leave no traces of me when I ran, because any hint of me could mean danger for those left behind.

I left the copy of Huck Finn for Slayer that he'd been reading but tore out the front page with my name scrawled on it in the loopy cursive handwriting of a young girl. I hated to leave it behind. That book had gotten me through a dozen foster families, but I hoped it would offer Slayer some of what it had given me over the years. I left nothing else lying around that belonged to me because a life of temporary living had taught me to be tidy, or as Vivi said, tidy made getting the hell out easier.

Thirty minutes later, the car was packed again, and I was behind the wheel trying to decide where to go. I could be in Mexico in a few hours but crossing the border meant cameras and official ID, exactly what I didn't need at the moment. No, I couldn't run without a plan, but I couldn't stay here with Maisie.

I glanced around to make sure there were no eyes watching before I started the engine and pulled out of my spot to drive away from the bunkhouse. I intended to leave Hardtail ranch in my rearview mirror. The southern edge of the property was under construction so that exit was out of the question. Most of the official ranch business took place on the west side of the property, which left the north end unoccupied. More importantly, undisturbed.

I came to a break in the road, a small dirt path that I hoped would take me to a spot where I could stay for a few days. Maybe without any distractions I could come up with a workable plan to disappear. In fact, maybe it was time to do things old school.

It was time to get out on the streets and get shit done. Time to go analog.

Chapter Eleven

Gunnar

"All done, Gunny!" Maisie raised her sticky, syrup-covered hands in the air and wiggled her fingers with a giggle. "It was yummy, Miss Martha!"

The older woman beamed down at Maisie's smiling face, tweaking her nose before she set a few more biscuits in the bowl at the center of the table. "I'm glad you liked it, sweetheart."

"Where is Peaches?" A full day had passed since the woman had shown her face on the ranch, and I was starting to think maybe she'd given me what I had silently begged for, her early departure.

"Don't know, maybe she's busy." I hoped that whatever kept her busy also kept her away. My body still tingled for her and yeah, I couldn't stop thinking about the way she felt under my hands, under my body, clenched around my cock while I pumped into her.

That one time hadn't been enough and that just fucking pissed me off.

"Come to think of it, I haven't seen hide nor hair of her in more than a day." Martha's words were full of concern. I wanted to tell her it was unwarranted, but then she'd give me that disappointed look that I couldn't stand, and I was in too good a mood for that. "I sure hope she's all right."

The sound of the phone ringing in my office was like a lifeline, and I took off down the hall like I was being chased, smiling at the name flashing across my display screen. "Cross, man. How the hell are you?"

"Good to hear your voice, brother. Thought maybe you'd forgotten about us old Bastards." The smile in his voice matched my own, and I dropped down in the worn brown leather chair and kicked my feet up on the heavy wooden desk.

"Never. Had a few problems with one of my contractors so I've had to deal with that shit. This good ol' boy bullshit is getting on my nerves."

I didn't give a fuck whose uncle used to work on the land I now owned, and I didn't care how long someone's family had lived in the area. But everyone around here did and thought they could bully me into extra fees and licenses. "It's been a real fucking pleasure to show them how I do business."

Cross laughed and it was rich and deep, a real sign that being with Moon and her son had done wonders for him. Transformed him from a broken man into a complete one. The club was better for it, and I only hoped I would be half as good as he was.

"Wish I could've been a fly on the wall for that conversation," he said chuckling in his deep baritone.

"It wasn't pretty but I got my point across. How's shit up your way?" I knew Cross well, had served as his VP for years, and I knew this wasn't a personal call, at least not strictly personal.

"Quiet, which is good. And the money is steady so no complaints. But, ah, shit I just found out from Jag that Peaches might be headed your way."

I opened my mouth to tell him she'd already been annoying me for days, but he kept on talking. "She's got some bad motherfuckers looking for her."

"Yeah, what'd she do?" Women like her were nothing but trouble, and now I regretted letting her stay even one damn day.

"Nothing. She did a job for the Covert Affairs Division but she was strictly logistics, hacking CCTV and shit like that, no real clue what the target or job was. But someone sent her some footage accidentally." His emphasis on the word said he didn't believe it was an accident at all. "Now everyone who worked the job behind the scenes is dead and they tried to kill her too. Twice."

Shit. Goddamn. "Fuck me, Cross."

"Yeah, I know. Vivi didn't say anything to anyone until today, but she got worried you might turn her bestie away."

"And she batted her lashes for you to step in on her behalf?" Vivi was a solid chick, but she was a loud mouth and a know it all, two traits I hated in women.

"More like she asked for a favor, and I couldn't refuse, especially when she didn't even remind me just how much we all owed her." He was impressed with her for it, which meant I couldn't say no. "I know you left all this shit behind, Gunnar and believe me I wouldn't ask if there were any other options."

"The clubhouse wasn't an option?" Because it seemed like a place filled with armed veterans was as safe as the next one.

"Vivi is the only family she has. This is the first place they'll come looking. Believe me, we've been on alert here since we found out she'd been here and gone already."

"She's already here. Arrived a while ago and been annoying me the whole damn time."

The relief in his sigh made me feel guilty. These guys were my brothers, no matter what, and I wasn't ready to turn my back on a request for help because of a woman.

"Is she still there?"

"I haven't seen her today, but I'm sure she's in the bunkhouse, thinking of more ways to get under my fucking skin." She had a talent for getting me riled up faster than any woman I'd ever met. "I'll tell you what I told her; she can stay a few days, but I have a child to think about, Cross."

"We'd appreciate if you'd do what you can." His voice had cooled, and I could hear the distance there. He was pissed.

Yeah, well, so was I. "Why in the hell do you even care about this chick?"

"She pitched in to help us for no other reason than Vivi is family, and she's too damn stubborn to ask anyone else for help. I figured if she came to you…never mind. I'll figure something out. It was good to hear your voice, brother." The call ended just like that.

"Dammit!" Peaches was nothing but trouble. Even when she wasn't around Peaches was causing trouble in my life.

"Everything all right, Boss?" Slayer stood in the office doorway looking intimidating as fuck with his dark features, thick beard and permanent scowl on his face.

"Not even a fucking little bit. You need something?"

"Yeah." His gaze swung up and down the hall before he stepped inside. "I didn't say anything at first because I didn't know what her deal was but—"

Christ would this woman twist up every man in her orbit? "What the fuck did she do now?"

"Nothing." Slayer flashed a grin and leaned forward on his elbows. "When we came home the night before last, she was gone, and I didn't think anything of it, figured she's entitled to her life as much as the rest of us. But she wasn't there last night and all her stuff is gone. Plus she left this behind but she tore the front page out." He held a book up with the page open so I could see the jagged edges of a torn page.

"And?"

"Why would she just leave like that? Is she all right?"

"People leave Slayer. Besides, she was only meant to stay a few days anyway." I wished like hell I could ignore the worry in his eyes but dammit, if this battle hardened warrior was worried, I couldn't.

"Yeah, but she left when we were all gone, and she didn't say goodbye." He sighed and pointed to the book again. "She's had this book since she was a kid, said it was the only thing other than unhealthy coping mechanisms she'd gotten out of foster care."

"Ah, fuck! Fuckity fuck!" So much for a relaxing day cracking heads over at the Barn Door to make sure the club was on track. Opening day was in six weeks, and I wouldn't accept anything less. "She leave a note or something?"

Slayer shook his head. "Not a trace that she'd ever even been there. Not a pink razor or a stray hair, which was suspicious on its own."

She was running. Again. And I couldn't help but feel like it was my fault. I should be happy to be rid of her, but knowing how serious her trouble was, guilt settled over me like a goddamn dark cloud. "Thanks for letting me know."

"Not a problem, Gunner. Just thought you should know. Later, man."

Now I had to figure out what the fuck to do about Peaches.

***

"I don't want any more goddamn excuses, just get this shit done!" If one more contractor stood in front of me and delivered more bad news, I would kill them all, bury them under the land and then torch it all to hell. "You said it would be finished by the end of the week unless the weather turned bad. You've had plenty of times to meet that deadline, and there's nothing but sunshine ahead. Get it done or get the fuck out." Staring at the waste of human space, I dared him to make another fucking excuse.

"My granddaughter's communion is Friday."

"Not my problem. Finish the job when you said you would, or we'll settle this in court. I've been more than patient with you Griff."

"You have."

"This is my business and if you can't stick to your word then I'll find someone who can." Griff seemed like a nice guy but had too many excuses and it seemed like everyone just let him get away with it. Before he could tell me another damn sob story, I walked off, meeting Saint outside where he sucked on a cigarette.

"How'd things go with Griff?"

"He's fucking with me, right?" That was the only reasonable explanation, this whole goddamn town was screwing with me to get me to leave.

"Griff's harmless, but I think he's a little too used to low expectations." Saint replied.

I wanted to ask him why the fuck he hired the guy then, but it was pointless. If Griff didn't come through, I'd hire the next guy. "Everything else coming along?"

"Yep. If Griff meets his deadline, we can start putting the inside together Tuesday or Wednesday next week."

My shoulders visibly relaxed. "That's good news." The kid still wouldn't look me in the eye, but I was getting used to the scared kitty routine. Almost. "What's your story?"

He shrugged, green eyes dancing everywhere but my face. "No story. Went into the Army right out of high school, had a special talent for weapons and they fostered that in the service. Shit went bad, lost some guys and now my head's all fucked up. End of story."

I should have recognized the signs sooner. Max had spent years walking around like a goddamn zombie, only unlike Joplin, he wasn't afraid of his own shadow. "You seein' someone about it?"

He shook his head. "Nah, it's fucking useless, you know?"

"That's what everyone thinks. Until they get to the other side." It sounded trite, but it also had the benefit of being true. "Listen, I need to know you can handle your shit when this place is packed, the music is pumping and lights are flashing all around you." I saw the moment the lightbulb went on in his head.

"Got it, Boss. I'll be ready, I promise."

"Good. You need to take care of yourself."

"Right. Thanks Gunnar." His gaze was a little cagey, but I understood better so I didn't say anything. "I'll let you know how things are going. Have you found Peaches yet?"

"No." Not that I'd spent a lot of effort looking for her, but so far, she hadn't popped up in any of the hotels or B&B's in Opey or the surrounding cities. Cross hadn't called again and that made me feel like a bigger piece of shit, like he knew he couldn't count on me once I left Vegas behind. "Shit. I'll see you around Saint."

Dropping onto the ATV I'd taken out of the barn that morning, I looked out at the land. Today was a little cloudy, but it didn't take away from the beauty or the vastness of the ranch. No, that was the task ahead of me. Riding around the whole damn ranch, because I told Holden I wanted to do it myself, to make sure there were no downed fences, no squatters or stray animals. There was something about riding around the property with the wind and sun on my face. It was almost like having a bike between my legs while it ate up the road.

Almost.

From the section dedicated to The Barn Door, I headed west toward the southern pasture, which was bare right now so the grass could replenish before we moved the cattle again. Nothing was out of order, and I let myself enjoy being outdoors as I rode around the property, giving the cattle in the west pasture a wide berth just in case they thought I might mean their calves harm. I didn't know a hell of a lot about animals, and I didn't want to learn about them today.

The northern pasture was unused and overgrown and I stopped for a few minutes when, my thoughts wandered to Peaches and the way she felt in my arms. Damn, that girl has some soft skin. Just like a lady should. She was wild and wicked—completely in the moment. It was hot as hell. It was goddamn unforgettable and thoughts of her, from the way she smelled to the way she moved, invaded my head making me wonder how she'd look completely naked and laid out on my bed. With my cock slipped between those lush lips of hers.

"Dammit."

I had to get a grip. Peaches was long gone and thinking about her was about as fruitful as thinking about a goddamn mermaid. I hadn't smoked a cigarette since Maisie came to live with me, but I wished I had one now. I needed something to calm my nerves.

I took off again and scanned the tall green bushes, thinking, and saw a small red triangle that had me off my ATV and closing the distance on foot. It was a tent, which could only mean a squatter. I slid my every day

9mm from my waist and called out, "Hey, anyone over here?"

I didn't expect an answer but the air grew still and the hairs on the back of my neck stood up. Someone was here.

"Hello?"

In the clearing I found not only a tent but also a small camp, complete with a fire pit and a camping pot. "This is private property," I called out, "so if you leave now, we won't have any problems."

"Seems like all we have are problems," a familiar, husky voice called out.

"Peaches? What the fuck are you doing out here?" I slid my gun back into its holster. Fuck. She stepped out of the tent and crossed her arms, glaring at me like I was the enemy.

"I was honoring the spirit of our agreement if not the actual words. Guess it's time to move on." She shrugged and scanned the area, quickly packing up her things. "I'll be gone soon."

"We've been looking all over for you." That brought her up, short but instead of gratitude there was disbelief on her face.

"Let me guess, you looked everywhere except this one spot where I was the entire time?" It was a rhetorical question I guessed, since she turned around and expertly disassembled the tent, folding it quickly and shoving it into a nylon bag.

"What were you doing out here?"

"Planning."

This damn woman was determined to make me lose my shit. "Not good enough."

She nodded, wild curls blowing in the breeze. "Doesn't matter. I'm leaving now." I knew she didn't want to leave, but to her credit, Peaches didn't go for theatrics and she didn't linger, packing her car quickly before she returned to clean up her campsite.

"Where will you go?"

She shrugged. "I'll land somewhere safe. See you around, Gunnar."

"Cross says you're in trouble." I blurted out.

When Peaches smiled it was like a rainbow after a storm, even the sad one she flashed over her shoulder. "Nothing I can't handle. Kiss Maisie for me."

"Stay here."

"Thanks, Gunnar, but I can't. Someone I sort of knew back east was found dead. They killed him, and he didn't know anything, not even my real name." She blinked, faster and faster until her tears were under control.

"I can't let you leave, Peaches."

"You can't make me stay either." She ducked inside the car and slammed the door loud enough that a few birds flew from their perch in the trees above us.

She was wrong about one thing, though. I could make her stay. Making my way to the driver's side, I tapped on the window. "I need your help."

"Don't lie to me, Gunnar and please don't make me start thinking you're a good guy."

My lips twitched at her smart fucking mouth. "Wouldn't dream of it. I do need the help, and since you're here, I'm figuring maybe I could get the friends and family discount."

Here burgundy brows arched and she leaned forward to look me in the eyes. "Are we friends, Gunnar?"

"We're not enemies." No matter what she thought, Peaches was not my enemy.

"Good to know. I still can't stay."

"Damn stubborn woman." I reached inside the window and snatched the keys from the ignition. "No one who knows you're here will tell anyone, which means you can stick around a few days to help me with my security for the club."

"I don't need your charity."

"Good, because nothin' in this life is free, sweetheart. You're getting room and board plus the best protection money can buy all for the low, low price of giving me the best security system you can."

"What kind of club?" She was intrigued and that was enough for now.

"Let's talk about it over dinner."

"Let's talk about it right now. Right here." Chin tilted in defiance, Peaches leaned back against the seat with her arms folded, giving me a perfect view of her tits. "What kind of club?"

"Adult entertainment. I need high end, non-intrusive digital security. That's your thing isn't it?"

"It is. One sign of trouble, and I'm out of here, whether the job is done or not. And don't ask for details. The less you know the better."

She was such a damn contradiction. Her curves and wild hair made her seem like a ditz or a sexpot, but she was smart as hell, capable and confident. It was a goddamn turn on. "I'll drive your car back to the house. I can send someone out here for the ATV. You can stay with me and Maisie."

"That's not a good idea. And I'll drive."

"Afraid you won't be able to keep your hands off me?"

"Maybe," she admitted, full lips curved into a sardonic smile and I jumped in the passenger seat and spent the drive back to the main house with a hard-on that made it impossible to think straight.

Chapter Twelve

Peaches

"So when you said adult entertainment you meant fucking."

I'd spent all night trying to figure out just who the hell Gunnar was, a nice guy trying to help a girl out of the goodness of his heart or a dick just like all the others. I was sure the job was just a way to get me to stick around a little longer to soothe his conscious or some fucked up shit like that.

Then this morning after a delicious breakfast of bacon, shoestring potatoes and fruit salad, Gunnar had grunted at me. "Come with me."

I decided not to be difficult for a change. After all, he'd given me a bedroom in the main house, upstairs near Maisie's room. In my trusty lace-up black boots I stomped out of the kitchen and followed him out of the main house with my eyes glued to his ass because…hell, the man did wicked things to denim. And denim did wicked things for his ass.

"Yeah, I meant fucking. You got a problem with that?" He was defensive, as he always was when it came to me, arms crossed and a scowl on his face in anticipation of my answer.

"No. I thought maybe I'd pegged you wrong. You don't strike me as a nightclub kind of guy, drink minimums and electronic music probably piss you off." Even the thought of it made me laugh because there were a lot of things that pissed Gunnar off. Even a damn fine orgasm hadn't cured him of his quick to anger reflex, and I didn't know whether to be insulted or accept it as the challenge my body seemed to think it was. "But this is exactly what I expected." The place still had a long way to go before the doors could open, but what was here looked hot.

"What the hell does that mean?" he asked me.

Another laugh bubbled up out of me and that laugh brought me up short. Gunnar was a grumpy son of a bitch, but dammit if he didn't always make me laugh. Whether he liked it or not. "It means that an adult club is dark and raw and gritty. Intense. That's more your speed."

"Hmph." He practically snarled in my direction before turning away, giving me a chance to look at the main room without his masculine distraction. I shouldn't have fucked him because now my body was like a whore in heat, too eager to climb that big body and go for another ride.

The main room was mostly an open space, and I could practically see it with the large hooks in the ceiling holding human-sized birdcages, reds and blacks everywhere with a thumping erotic beat filling the room. It had doors everywhere, mirrors too. Down a long dimly lit hall there was another room, twice as large as the first with a six-foot-high stage that was large enough to fit three king sized beds. At least. I let out a low whistle as I took it all in. "Wow."

"Impressed?"

"Kind of. This room just begs you to get naked and start fucking." It just had that vibe about it. Or at least it would soon.

"Let's go." At the back of the room he'd put in a spiral staircase with a cushioned velvet bannister I followed Gunnar down to a lower level. It was dark, and I knew the music would be a low throb, enough to mimic the race of the heartbeat as people walked the hallway, deciding which room to enter. The one with the mirrors so they could watch or be watched, the leather straps so they could get spanked or do the spanking, whips, ties, ball gags, silk scarves and pretty much anything else anyone with a kink could ask for was down here, the equipment very nearly complete.

The décor was dark jewel tones, deep blues and purples, red and green. Silk and velvet and leather. It all screamed sex.

"Well done," I said at the end of the tour.

It wasn't my first sex club, truth be told, but it was nicer than most. "You're expecting big money clients."

"I am."

"It shows. This place screams high end eroticism." Rich people had their kinks as much as the average guy, but money has a way of taking a kink and turning it on its ass.

"Glad you approve." His tone said he didn't give a damn, but I could see his relief as the tension in those broad shoulders relaxed.

"I do. When do you plan on opening the Back Door?"

His lips twitched. "Barn Door."

"Is that name negotiable?"

"Nope."

I shrugged. "Can't blame a girl for trying. Ready to talk business?"

His nod was reluctant but his blue gaze seared through me as we went through each room, one by one, and I gave him the lowdown on security. "Typically if you have a members only policy you don't need to worry about digital security in each room, not to mention you'll run afoul of porn laws if you do."

"Porn laws?"

I nodded. "Identification for performers and age verification, all that legal stuff that applies when you're shooting sex acts for profit." I knew he was about to insist it wasn't for profit. "It's not an accusation, just what the law will say if you're ever unfortunate enough to have to deal with them down here."

"So no cameras in the rooms? Just the hallways and the big rooms upstairs." His tone was firm, resolved. It surprised me because he seemed like a guy who would rather bite off his own arm than admit a woman was right. Especially me.

"Yep. Facing the big crowds, not the stage."

Gunnar nodded and scrubbed a hand down his scruff, drawing my attention to his thick-corded forearms dusted with dark hair. His head had been shaved clean when I saw him in Mayhem, but with short dark hair, he was even hotter. Bastard.

"Anything else?"

There was plenty and I figured it was best to get it all out of the way now, since he wouldn't be any more receptive to it another time.

"You should have quality cameras in the parking lot, at the front door, and on all sides of the building exterior. If some of these good ol' boys find out what this is and can't get in, you'll be happy for them."

He thought about my words for so long I thought he'd disregard them, hell I expected it. But he eventually nodded his agreement at the bottom of the stairs and motioned for me to go first.

"Thanks."

I blinked once. Twice. "Did you just…I'm sorry could you repeat that?" I stepped closer and leaned my ear toward him, enjoying the way his face lit up when he smiled because it happened so rarely.

"I said thank you, Peaches. Do you need it in writing?"

"Would you give it to me if I said yes?"

He took a step closer. "Nope."

"Tease," I accused and thought better of it a second too late. Gunnar was in my space, invading my space and my senses until my nipples were hard and my panties were soaked. My breathing was shallow, and I blamed his nearness, his cologne, that fucking gleam in his eyes.

"I never tease." His deep voice rumbled and even though my mind begged my body to take a step back, the dirty slut took a step forward until my nipples rubbed up against his hard chest under that soft t-shirt. Big hands slid down to my ass and pulled me up close and personal with his denim-clad erection just as his mouth slammed down on mine.

I didn't want his kiss, but damn if the rest of me did. I melted when our tongues collided and danced, but it wasn't a light and easy kiss. It wasn't breezy or casual, it was raw. It was hungry and all consuming, and I grabbed onto his big shoulders and hung on as my legs gave out under me.

When I moaned into Gunnar's mouth, he smiled and lifted me up with his big hands gripping my ass until I moaned again. It didn't matter that he slammed my back against the wall, all that mattered was the feel of his muscles under my hands, the taste of his tongue, the feel of his soft strong lips moving against mine. The way his cock nestled right between my thighs and made me wish we were both naked.

"Hey, Gunnar, you around?" The voice belonged to the only one of the men who didn't have much to say to me. Joplin Saint.

Gunnar froze and ground into me again, swallowing another of my moans before he stepped back and my legs slid to the floor. "Horrible fucking timing."

My body agreed, but my mind was grateful to the quiet, nervous man. "Perfect fantasy material for later," I told him and took a step back to straighten my shirt and smooth my untamable curls.

"Later?" he asked.

I wouldn't let the incredulity in his tone get to me.

"I'm coming up now!" he called up to Saint.

I went up first, giving Gunnar time to get that big cock of his under control, all while my body cried that he wasn't pounding into me right now.

"Hey Saint, how's it going?" I said lightly when we reached the top of the staircase.

He shrugged. "It's going. The club is coming along, don't you think?"

I spent a few minutes telling him my thoughts on the club. "Looks like this is a job that will keep you busy."

"Yeah, probably." His piercing green eyes looked everywhere but at me, and I gave him a small, not too friendly smile and walked away. Gunnar had the blueprints for the club so I could use them to give him a proper security plan.

At least a few hours of work would distract me from the fact that once again, I was a woman without a home.

Chapter Thirteen

Gunnar

"Are you sure you wanna do this?" Holden sat in the old green office chair that looked like it hadn't been replaced since the seventies, legs crossed on one side of the desk, Stetson covering the keyboard and his hands cupping the back of his head.

I sighed and looked around his office located in the back of the barn closest to the main house. "Hell no, I'm not sure, but it has to be done." I'd talked to Cross several times about an idea I'd been playing with since agreeing to let the guys come stay on the ranch. Finally, he agreed. "Do you think it's too soon?"

Holden shook his head, overgrown brown hair brushing up against his collar, not that I gave damn, but he always wore a hat so it was hard to tell what the hell he looked like.

"Nah. Sometimes a man just needs some support to heal, maybe this club will do that."

Right. "Here they come." The men, Saint, Slayer and Cruz, walked inside and took an empty seat without being told.

"What's going on, Boss?" Slayer leaned back in his chair with one leg crossed at the knee while he stroked his beard.

"It's Gunnar, and there are a few things we need to discuss." Other than Saint, all the men were relaxed and open to listening.

"Whatever it was, I didn't do it," Cruz said with a smile that was more innocent than he'd ever been in his whole fucking life.

"Yeah right." We all laughed at Cruz, who had a gift for not taking life too seriously. "First, we have another man coming soon. His name is Wheeler and he's bringing his brother, Mitch, with him. He's a therapist and I want you to feel free to talk to him if you feel you need to, but it isn't conditional on you staying here."

Men—especially military men—tended to have a certain view about admitting any kind of medical weakness, but they were out of the service now, and I needed them healthy. Looking around at each man, they each carried a certain type of pain and none of it was the same. Some guys had pain from their lives before picking a branch of the military and others carried the burden of what they'd seen and the things they'd been tasked with doing. For an unlucky few, the pain was two-fold.

"I hope Hardtail Ranch is as good for you as it has been for me, so if you need something that I can help with, I will try my damnedest to do just that."

They were a captive audience, but I wasn't fooling myself. It wasn't the message at all. Right now it was the fact that I'd given each of them a soft place to land when the military no longer had a use for them. For now, that was enough. "When I spoke to each of you as your time in the service drew to a close, you said you wanted to be part of something similar. A brotherhood. A family."

"Fuck yeah," Slayer smacked the table with a gleam in his eye.

"My friend and old Prez has given us the green light for an Opey, TX Chapter of the Reckless Bastards. You don't have to decide right, now but just know that's a discussion for another time." Holden, Slayer and even Cruz had that same gleam in their eyes that I had when I met Cross and some of the old timers who were still around back when I joined. A new family, a new adventure. It was exciting the same way basic training had been. And their first tour. Before the reality of the shitshow started to sink in.

"I'm in," Cruz said simply and I nodded my acknowledgment.

"This next piece of business is serious, but it has nothing to do with what we just talked about, got me?" I looked at each of them, making sure they all understood that helping me with this wouldn't change a thing.

"Got it," Slayer said easily.

"Yep," Holden added and smacked his cowboy hat on top of his head.

"Sure, Boss." Saint's whispered words nearly got me to smile.

"I'm in either way, but yeah, got it." Cruz sat up straight, years of training coursing through his veins as he awaited orders.

"Peaches is a friend of one of my best friend's old lady. She helped our club when we were in a bind and now, she finds herself in trouble and in need of protection." Without giving away too many details, I told them all about the CAD and the video she'd inadvertently received.

"She came here because there's no tangible connection between us, but I haven't exactly been welcoming to her." It ate at me to have to admit that I'd treated a woman in need that way, but once I reminded myself how well women could lie, the guilt lessened.

"She doesn't want to stay," Holden guessed with a smirk. "I thought you were a dick because you liked her."

Slayer sat up straighter. "You mean we've all been keeping our distance thinkin' she's yours and she ain't? I call dibs."

My fists clenched at my sides and my nostrils flared. "There are no dibs!"

Holden was the first asshole to start laughing and Slayer joined next, soon they were all cracking their asses up. Even Saint. "He likes her but doesn't even realize it. Priceless." Holden smacked his hat against his thigh and let out a loud guffawing laugh. "If I had known."

"If you had known you would've roped her in with your monster cock?" Holden was hung and it was no secret, not with his conquests showing up begging for another ride on his beanstalk.

"Jealous, Cruz?"

"Fuck yeah, I am. But now that Peaches is free—"

"—She's not," I practically roared and the room fell silent.

"Good to know." Slayer stood and rubbed his hands together. "You're staking a claim and your girl needs help. What else?"

"I got her to stay by getting her to do some digital security for The Barn Door and then Hardtail Ranch but that won't last much longer. She can't leave until we figure out exactly who is trying to kill her and why."

"I'll put the word around town to keep an eye out for anyone who doesn't belong. Coming from a native, they'll understand." Holden grabbed his keys from the hook and left.

"Me and Cruz can keep an eye on Peaches. She won't question it," Slayer said and I wondered just how close he and Peaches were. Was she just playing me so I'd help her?

"I wanna say yes," Saint began, eyes focused intently on the ground. "But what if I can't?"

"You can," I assured him. The kid had a bad case of PTSD so I'd decided not to be a hardass, at least not too much of one. "Just keep your eyes peeled on the property for anyone who doesn't belong, who looks like military or feds. Report what you see. Got it?"

"Yeah," he nodded. "Thanks, Gunnar."

"No problem. Think about what I said, guys." They all nodded and less than a minute later the office was empty. I locked it up, walking back toward the big white main house with a grin.

Opey really was starting to feel like home. Maybe it was Martha's home cooked meals six days a week or maybe it was the peace and beauty of the land, I didn't know, but I felt more relaxed than I ever had in my life. Sometimes that peace made me resent Peaches for fucking it all up, but as much as I wanted to, I knew I couldn't turn her away.

Wondering what she was up to and what crazy, barely there outfit she'd have on, I ran up the front steps and entered the house, finding it dark and empty, which was odd for this time of day. Martha had gone to do some shopping, leaving Maisie with her daughters, which meant Peaches was likely lounging around somewhere half naked.

I didn't mean to eavesdrop but after pouring a tall glass of fresh lemonade, I went outside and sat down on the porch. Before long I heard a voice coming from inside that rooted me to the ground. "Where's your mommy and daddy, Peaches?"

She sighed, a sad wistful sound. "My mom is dead, and I don't remember her much because she was too sick to take care of me, and she never got around to telling me about my father. Where's yours?"

I clenched my teeth, angry with her for bringing up memories that Maisie didn't need to relive. I was tempted to go inside but my feet wouldn't move. "My mommy is dead, too but I have Gunny."

At least Maisie still loved being around me. Her sweet smile and those little girl kisses that always contained just a little too much slobber always made me feel ten feet tall. No one else in the fucking world had to like me as long as I had her love.

"You're a very lucky girl," Peaches told her seriously. "He's grumpy, but he loves you very much." I didn't know why hearing her say that hit me the way it did, but dammit, it made me proud to know someone could see it. I stepped up to the window to peer into the sunroom where they sat talking.

"I love Gunny too. He's the bestest big brother ever."

Peaches laughed at her exuberance, and I closed my eyes and let the sound wash over me. Warm me right along with the sun.

"For his sake, I hope you remember that when you're a teenager and he chases away all the boys who want to date you."

Maisie giggled. "I don't like boys."

"Smart chica. Boys are trouble, every last one of them." Her words— though playful—held a note of truth, and I wondered what her story was. Not enough to ask but just a general kind of curiosity.

"Even Gunny?" I could always count on Maisie to look out for me.

"Especially your precious Gunny."

I stepped back from the window with a smile that I was glad no one was around to witness. It was good to know Peaches was affected by me too. I turned away and ran right into Martha coming up the steps. "Hey, uh, Martha."

"Eavesdropping ain't nice, hon."

"Yeah, I know." There was no reason to deny what we both knew to be the truth.

"But you're infatuated and you can't help it, so eager to learn every little thing. I understand perfectly." I wanted to deny it but Martha smacked her lips and patted my chest. "You could try being nice. Women like that in a man." She walked into the house with her grocery bags and a knowing smile on her face, leaving me with nothing but thoughts of Peaches as I made my way up to the shower.

Alone.

The dream was damn near a reality, that was the only thing on my mind as I stood in front of the red and black barn and watched the guys raise the sign above the entrance. The twisted metal sign sat above the door, dramatic and welcoming. My fingertips tingled with excitement thinking about the club finally opening its doors.

Too excited to wait, I stepped inside and my shit-eating grin grew even wider. It looked like a club. A sensual place where adults could come to satisfy their sexual desires, explore different kinks in a safe, discreet environment. It was the perfect place to be on a Thursday night.

And it was all mine.

Inside Saint had his sleeves rolled up, helping screw leather cuffs to the walls because you never know when the mood to get bound and fucked would strike. The oversized bird cages sat on the floor, ready to be hoisted into the air the moment the doors opened. "Looking good, Saint!"

"Thanks Gun! We're so fucking close, man." It was the first real hint of excitement I'd seen from the kid since I arrived in Texas months ago.

Everything was coming together and the worry and stress I felt didn't seem quite so un-fucking-manageable anymore. The big bar up front was in place with black studded leather, and I knew there was a smaller matching bar in back. The jacuzzi room was set up, complete with big leafy trees and the stripper poles had already been installed in two of the private rooms.

Inside the security office, Peaches sat with our new security guard, Ford. He was barely on the right side of legal. He was a big motherfucker, at least six foot five with shoulders as wide as a goddamn hummer. He was a bear of man from the neck down, and fresh from the Army, which meant he could handle himself if the customers got a little too excited. And because he was tough, he wouldn't take any shit.

"How's it going in here?"

Peaches looked over her shoulder and arched a brow. "Excellent. Ford is a quick study, and he's already got the security system down."

I looked to Ford for confirmation, and he gave a discreet nod. "Glad to hear it."

"Can we talk a minute?" Peaches stood and shimmied her way out of the tiny room, careful that none of her touched me or Ford.

"Sure, what's up?"

"Security for the club and the property is set up, streaming to an external hard drive that only you have access to. Ford knows how to update, search footage and maintain day to day security, but I told him he could call if he needed help." She wrapped her arms around her body, completely unaware of how her t-shirt dress highlighted her curves. "I'll be out of here in two days, max."

"You can stay." It was just three small words but they felt monumental. Important. Too important for a chick I barely knew and only fucked once, though I couldn't deny how badly I wanted to fuck her again.

"We both know I can't do that, Gunnar." She gave the club one last sweeping look. "Your new life is shaping up just fine. Don't worry about me." She walked away, so confident and determined that she was leaving Hardtail Ranch.

If nothing else, I'd have fun watching her try.

Chapter Fourteen

Peaches

Packing up my shit took less than five minutes. Still I took my time, two days' time to be exact, so I could spend more time with Maisie before taking off, and maybe so I could just soak up being around people who were somewhat familiar to me. Who knew when I'd be surrounded by so many people again, especially people I could trust?

Enough time had passed and no one had been to my old apartment in weeks and if they'd somehow managed to bypass the surveillance system, then they could be closing in on me while I stood in the middle of the guest room gathering dust.

Time to get a move on, so I grabbed my backpack and laptop case first and set them beside the front door before making the trip back upstairs for two small boxes containing more digital equipment. All piled together by the door, it would seem that I'd acquired more things than I realized while I was here. Another sign it was time to move on.

With my keyring looped around my middle finger, I jogged down the stairs and made my way to the gravel square behind the bunkhouse where all the guys parked their rides.

Slayer's Harley sat in one corner, daring the other cars to get close enough to breath its air. Cruz's black pickup truck was shiny all over and parked at an angle to keep the paint job safe and clean. And then there was an unfamiliar black SUV parked exactly where my car should have been. "What the fuck?"

There was only one reasonable explanation and it had nothing to do with my car magically evaporating on its own. An angry thought that propelled me to retrace my steps and go in search of the overbearing jerk who ghosted my ride.

My boots were loud on the polished hard wood floors inside the main house but I didn't care. If Martha wanted to lecture me about her floors, she could get in line. I had a bigger problem at the moment. As I pushed the door open, I was vaguely aware of two additional people in the room, but they weren't my target. Yet. "You!" I pointed right at Gunnar and walked inside.

"Guys, this is Peaches, our resident expert in all things tech related." He smiled that easygoing smile that didn't come naturally to him, acting like this was just another regular day on the ranch.

"Yeah, hey, how ya doin' and all that." I pointed at Gunnar again, letting him know he wasn't going to get away with this. "Where the hell is my car, Gunnar?"

"Getting repaired." His big arms folded across his wide chest, and for just a second, my lady parts stood up and took notice of the tattoo on his right bicep, the dark hair dusting his forearms, and the mouthwatering bulge of his pecs.

"Bullshit. That car was in excellent condition when I arrived because I made sure of it. Return it. Now."

"Can't do that, Peaches. Vivi made me promise to keep you safe, and that means keeping you here."

A tortured sound, half growl and half groan, escaped from my throat, making the men stare at me.

"News flash Gunnar, my freedom and safety are no one's concern but mine. Not Vivi's and definitely not yours, no matter how much you both think otherwise."

His sigh revealed his frustration at my insistence, but I didn't care, not while he was being so fucking high-handed. "Yeah, we're the bad guys for wanting to keep you safe."

"No one said you were good or bad, but this isn't your choice. I'm leaving, the question is. . . will I fuck up your nice new security system before I do." We stared at each other for a long time, the air tense and charged between us.

One of the new arrivals bolted out of his chair and stepped forward, breaking the eye contact between us. "Hey, I'm Mitch and this is my brother, Wheeler."

I blinked a couple times to get rid of the anger, frustration and arousal coursing through my veins. "Nice to meet you Mitch. I'm Peaches." His handshake was warm and friendly, soft hands that said he wasn't a soldier or a tradesman. But Mitch and his brother looked a lot alike with dark hair and matching blue eyes.

His brother barely spared me a glance with his grunted greeting. "Yeah, hello."

Just what this place needed, another grouchy asshole to make me glad I was getting the hell out of here. "Just tell me where my car is and you can get back to your life, Gunnar." It didn't make sense, why he was being so obstinate about this.

"If you leave the ranch, no one will have your six, Peaches."

He was right about that, but it wasn't his concern, and that was how I preferred it. "I have my back, like always."

"Not good enough."

"Well that's too damn bad! Why do you even give a damn anyway? Last time I checked; you have a four-year-old kid you need to worry about. Not me."

Anger transformed his features back to the surly bastard I'd met back in Mayhem. His blue eyes were so dark they might as well have been obsidian. His face contorted into a kind of anger that made me take a step back and had Mitch moving between us once again. Gunnar smacked the large wooden desk with his fists. "You're not going anywhere. Don't test me on this."

"You can't win this, Gunnar. Either I go in the safety of my vehicle or take my chances on foot."

"Wanna bet?" There was a gleam in his eyes that I didn't trust and took another step back.

"Hey, let's calm down," Mitch said and I knew instantly he was a doctor. A head doctor. "We need to be calm. All of us."

"Stay out of it, Mitch." Wheeler stood beside his brother, a hand of solidarity on his shoulder. "Gunnar won't hurt her, this is a lover's spat."

"The hell it is," Gunnar snarled.

"Doesn't matter what it is because right now, it's over." I turned on my heels and stomped away like a child on the verge of a tantrum. I knew if I stayed I might do something crazy, like punch Gunnar's rugged face or choke him out. Either one sounded pretty good at the moment.

Upstairs, I glanced around the room in search of any items I might have left behind. It wouldn't do any good to leave any traces that I'd been here since it would only spell trouble for Gunnar and the people on the ranch. The door slammed behind me, startling the fuck out of me, and I turned, ready to fight. "Why the fuck are you so stubborn?"

"Because it pisses you off. Clearly." The man had it in his head that everything I did was to piss him off or ruin his day, but really it was just a happy coincidence. "That's the only reason I breathe, don't you know?"

His growl was pure frustration but dammit if my nipples didn't perk up at the sound. "You're safe here."

"Yeah and I appreciate that you give a damn about me, but I'm not your concern, Maisie is. The longer I stay here, the worse it will be if they find me."

"Let me worry about that."

I snorted at his typical male response. "Yeah and I'll just sit around eating bon bons, not giving a thought to the men out there trying to find me. You don't know where I've been, what I've seen. And I can't play little lady and let you and a bunch of vets worry about me, Gunnar." Although deep inside, I wished it was that easy.

"Worry your pretty little head all you want but do it here at Hardtail Ranch. You went to Vivi first, so clearly you understand how serious this is."

"I didn't go to Vivi for protection. She's the only family I've got, and as time goes by, she'd wonder why she hadn't heard from me. I went there to say goodbye, Gunnar."

"Well there's no need for that now, because you're staying." He was in my space, crowding me against the wall until he blocked out everything else.

"No, I'm not." Our gazes collided for a few seconds, so much fire and anger and energy between us that it was hard to ignore. Even harder to ignore was our shallow breathing, the charged air between us. The anticipation.

Gunnar acted first, spearing his fingers through my curls so he could hold my head in the perfect position to accept his kiss, and what a fucking kiss it was. Hot and hard, the kind of kiss that let a woman know just how wanted she was. His kiss told me more than Gunnar would ever say or let me see, how much he craved me. How badly he desired me, and how frustrated he was that he couldn't have me.

Being on the other side of his maleness was as intoxicating as I remembered and I submitted to his kisses, his frantic touches, like he was trying to memorize it all for later. Our kiss lasted so long I forgot where I was and what we were arguing about until finally, Gunnar pulled back with sleepy smiling blue eyes. "You feel as good as I remember," he growled and pressed his lips to my neck, my collarbone, the spot on my neck that made my panties wet in mere seconds.

I tried to push out the sound of his voice and focus only on the way he made me feel, but Gunnar liked to talk.

"So fucking soft," he moaned after making quick work of my tank top and bra, groaning and making incoherent noises while his mouth did delicious things to my tits. He sucked and kissed, nibbled and licked until I writhed against him, fingers thrust through his short hair so I could hold him close, keep him right where I wanted him.

"Gunnar." The moan slipped out but I felt too good to think about what it meant when he released me with a loud pop. His mouth was easily one of my favorite things about him, when it was silent, anyway.

"What is it?" His words came out on a pant, his dark eyes unable to look away from my tits, nipples hard and aching without his mouth on them. "Tell me what you want, Peaches."

"What I want Gunnar, is for you to taste me." His response was to lift me in the air like I weighed nothing, spin and drop me onto the freshly made bed. I watched him through heavy lidded eyes as desire licked up my flesh. In one short move my shorts were on the floor and my panties were in his hand and I watched, totally fucking turned on, as he inhaled the scent of me.

"Fuck, I can't wait to taste you." Then without hesitation, Gunnar sank down on his knees and pulled me to the edge of the bed, spreading my legs wide to accommodate his broad shoulders. He inhaled deeply and let out a purely masculine growl before his mouth was on me, licking slowly at first and then faster, with flicks of the tongue added that drove me out of my fucking mind.

My hips bucked and rolled against him but Gunnar held me down, tasting me like I was his favorite menu item at the best restaurant in town. His hands gripped my thighs so I couldn't move while his mouth and tongue worked me like an expert. "Fuck, Gunnar!"

His deep chuckle rumbled against me, sending vibrations through my whole body until all I could do was pant and curse and seek out more and more pleasure. "Not yet," he growled as his finger slipped inside me and hit that spot that temporarily stole all body functions.

"Gunnar, I'm close," I warned.

"I know. Not yet," he demanded and wrapped his lips around my clit, sucking and nibbling until my orgasm was beyond the stopping point. "Now," he growled and sucked hard, while his fingers pumped into me harder and deeper, until my orgasm nearly drowned him.

"Oh, fuck!" The words came out a long, low cry as pleasure shot through my body, making it quiver until it tightened almost painfully. "Fuck. Shit. Oh, God!"

I was vaguely aware of his laughter but my body was too damn satisfied to care, especially when his cool tongue hit my hot, sensitive clit. "Such a sweet little pussy."

"Have another serving if you want," I told him as shivers wracked my body every time his breath fanned my wetness. "Or you could give me what we both want." Gunnar stood at my words and undressed like a teenager on prom night, giving me a long moment to take in the beauty that was his body. His skin wasn't smooth and perfect, it was scarred with knife wounds, gunshots and tattoos. The story of his life written in his flesh.

"Yeah, what is it that I want?"

Silly man. Like I didn't know. "I have an idea." Because it was just what I wanted, and I would get it how I needed it, hard and dirty. Rolling over, I pushed up on all fours, giving him a tantalizing view of my ass and my dripping wet pussy. "Looks a little like this?"

Gunnar growled and rubbed two fingers down my pussy, groaning at how wet I still was. Or was again, who could tell at the moment? "Just like that."

"Don't make me wait." I wasn't in the mood for games or teasing. My body was so aroused, I could barely form words, choosing instead to wiggle my ass in front of him.

The sound of his growl filled with nothing but male appreciation sent another rocket of desire through my body. Then the feel of his tongue circling my asshole nearly had my legs and arms giving out. Gunnar smacked my ass and before I could protest his cock was invading my space, stretching me out deliciously from this angle. "Oh fuck."

His cock was hard as steel and his grip would leave bruises in the morning but this was one hell of a send-off and I planned to fully enjoy it. "That's the idea, big guy. Fuck me. Hard."

After that, the only sound in the room was slick skin smacking against slick skin as he rammed me from behind, hard and deep. His cock felt even longer and thicker from this angle and my back arched on its own so I could take those final two inches. "Shit!"

I smiled because I knew exactly how he felt. It was incredible, too fucking good and all I could do was dig my hands and knees into the mattress and brace myself. The onslaught of his strokes was almost overwhelming in their speed and frequency, the intensity of how he used his body to bring us both pleasure. "Gunnar, yes! Oh fuck yes!"

His name fell from my lips like a prayer, and it seemed to push him more. Gunnar's hips moved with lightning speed, the force of his body dislodging a second orgasm I didn't expect so soon after the first. Two of my fingers made their way between my legs, rubbing my clit with a wild abandon while Gunnar fucked me from behind, one slick finger sliding between my ass cheeks and right into that bundle of nerves. "Fuck you're tight everywhere."

Pride warred with desire but then something happened. It was all too much, the feel of his finger in my ass, his cock stretching and pounding into me, my fingers on my clit. It was too much and my extremities quivered as pleasure worked its way to the surface. "Gunnar," I warned. "Gunnar!"

"Let go," he roared as his own cock grew even harder inside of me until I was completely full. Of him. Seconds later I was flat on my face, body shaking violently as my orgasm tore through me. But Gunnar was no joke, still holding my hips, he fucked me hard and fast until every drop of orgasm seeped from his body—and mine. "Holy fucking shit."

A smile spread at his words because what else was there to say after sex that powerful and intense? "Yeah, that."

His body collapsed on top of mine for just a second before he pulled me close and curled himself around my back. "You're still not leaving."

"We both know I have to. Don't make this harder than it has to be, all right?" It was a sad truth, but even that incredible orgasm couldn't distract me from the fact that this fuck was nothing more than a drawn out goodbye.

***

"That fucker took my car, can you believe it?" I stood outside the main house in a field far enough away from the house that no one could hear me.

Vivi groaned on the other end of the call. "Where in the hell do you think you're gonna go girl? Be reasonable."

"I am, Vivi. You think I want to be on the run with no clue where I'm gonna sleep from one night to the next? Well I don't, okay? But he's got a kid here, Vivi. The most adorable little girl in the whole world and she deserves a good life without the shit we've had to deal with. Right?" Why in the hell did I have to keep explaining myself to people?

"Clearly, you're on Gunnar's side about this so I don't know why I even called."

She let out a disbelieving snort and even though I couldn't see the smartass, I knew she was rolling her eyes at me. "You called because you needed someone to talk some damn sense into your head. You need to stay where you are and let us keep doing what we're doing."

"Which is what, exactly?" I hadn't heard from her in more than a week, another reason I needed to get going.

"No one can find Bob again. Jag has reached out to some of his contacts back east and even Stitch reached out to some of his buddies who now do private contracting work." She sighed again, her frustration with this situation evident in that one little puff of air. "We need to find, Bob, but that's not all."

I didn't like that tone. "No way Vivi. Don't even fucking think it."

"You know it's the only way."

"Find another way. There is no way in hell I'm letting you see that fucking video, the bane of my goddamn existence and the reason people are trying to kill me. No. Fucking. Way." I would do just about anything for her, my sister from another mister, but I wouldn't put her life in danger. Not for this.

"You're getting sentimental in your old age if you're worried about me. We both know I'm the tough one anyway."

"Bullshit," I gasped. "You're the one who freaked out after we hacked that DEA stash house and tried to become Canadian."

"Hey," she laughed and the sound was sweet and familiar down the line. "We could've had free healthcare all this time if you had only listened to me."

"I was in, but you didn't want to go get the money. How were we gonna live?" That place had millions of dirty dollars in it and Vivi had chickened out at the last minute. "You didn't want to do that and I understood and stayed, so we could stay together."

She groaned. "That's dirty as hell and you know it."

"I do." There was no point pretending to be apologetic when we both knew I wasn't sorry at all.

"Good. Then you won't get mad when I tell you that I'm knocked up and I'm pulling out the big guns. I can't worry about you out there running for your life from God only knows who and grow this genius baby at the same time."

"A baby? Fuuuuck." Whenever we got our hands on pot or booze as kids, Vivi and I would try to imagine this part of our lives. "You're doing it, Vivi. Becoming a normy."

She snorted. "Hell, I hope not. My baby daddy is a biker and a hacker, that's not all that normal. Is it? Tell me it's not normal, Peaches."

"Aww, you're nervous. That's adorable. And totally fucking normal." At that little squeak of outrage, I laughed like I hadn't laughed in a long damn time. This chick was my family. My center. "You went even better than becoming a normy. You went and fell in love with a weirdo just like you. Can you imagine what your kid's gonna be like?"

"Ugh, this baby is turning me into a pussy." She sniffled and continued to curse her hormones while I laughed my ass off. "You really think this is a good thing?"

"I really do. Your baby will be wicked smart and able to kick some ass. Not to mention all those badass uncles lurking around." That was the nice thing about being in Mayhem, there was plenty of man candy to ogle. But they were in the middle of a war and grumpy as fuck so they were purely eye candy whereas the men on Hardtail Ranch were people.

I hated when that happened.

"Yeah that's true." Her tone was wistful, and I knew she was still struggling with her emotions. Neither of us were too big on showing emotions, particularly any that might show even a hint of vulnerability. Even now. "Please stay there Peaches. I want you here when this baby comes out of me, just in case."

Damn. Goddamn motherfucker! I stared around at Hardtail Ranch drenched in moonlight, and I sighed. This place wasn't so bad but staying here left me feeling antsy and anxious. "I really hate that I fuckin' love you right now Vivi."

She laughed. "I know and I'm okay with that. I'm not sure I can do this without you, Peaches. Seriously."

"Fine, I'll stay. But don't say I didn't warn all of you when the shit goes bad." Everyone would blame me, of course, and only then would I get to walk away.

"*If* it goes bad," she said firmly. "Maybe it won't. No one knows you're there, and they won't find out from any of us."

I wanted to believe that, more than anything in this world, but the pragmatic part of me wouldn't shut up. "Unless they somehow figure out that one of the Reckless Bastards recently left and moved to the middle of nowhere. Otherwise, you're right, totally safe."

"Damn, life on the run has turned you into a cynic."

That tore a bitter laugh from me. "Being a cynic is why I'm still alive."

"That and Gunnar. Let him protect you or I'll name this kid Chip or Trevor, maybe Chad."

"You wouldn't dare. Jag will name him something like binary or CSS."

"I miss your crazy ass."

"Ditto, kiddo." It had taken me years to get used to Vivi's easy words of love and until I did, I would say those words to her.

She laughed. "Next time we talk you better be calling me from a new phone." The call ended abruptly, and I quickly removed the SIM card and dismantled the phone as best I could. Tomorrow I would melt it down and toss it in the scrap heap behind the barn.

For now, I needed to think. And sleep. But mostly think about what Vivi said. She was having a baby and wanted me reachable, but that meant putting all of the people here in danger.

I didn't like it, but for now, I would stay put.

Chapter Fifteen

Gunnar

"What do you guys think?" This was the surprise I'd been working on ever since word came down from Cross about setting up a new Reckless Bastards chapter in Texas. It was a gift of sorts for all of us, for the future we would have as a family. As brothers.

Slayer strolled into The Barn Door first, his hair hanging free because the man enjoyed looking like he just rolled out from between a woman's thighs.

"This place is a wet fucking dream, Gunnar." He looked around as he entered, taking his time walking up the left side of the large table with the leather studded center, letting his fingers graze over the finish. Eventually it would have the chapter name emblazoned on it. When the time was right. "This shit is tight, man."

"At the risk of agreeing with this big fucker, this is dope, Gunnar." Cruz, with his hands shoved in his pockets, looked around with a satisfied smile. Cruz played shit close to the vest, which I respected in a brother in arms.

"All we need is a naked woman draped over this table with her mouth wide open." Slayer grabbed his junk and howled.

"Better be Holden's cock going in her mouth," Wheeler smiled and punched Holden on the arm as they entered together. "Since his cock 'was the first time I ever enjoyed choking on it'." His voice was pitched high like a woman's, making everyone laugh.

"Can I help it if Kiki is a freak?" Holden's shit-eating grin said he loved having a woman show up and brag about his monster cock. What man wouldn't? "She choked herself on it, I simply enjoyed what she offered."

Wheeler clapped him on the back with a loud barking laugh. The two had become fast friends, easily working the ranch together without any problems. "Can't say I blame you at all, man." He turned to me and silently asked if he could take a seat. "It seems like we all wanna do this thing Gunnar, what do we have to do?"

A slow smile spread across my face and it was a feeling I was starting to get used to again. I hadn't spent much time laughing and smiling over the past few years because it took all my energy just to look after Maisie and keep things normal while we were at war. Constant fucking war.

"That will come in time." This place and these men were starting to feel like home. Not the old home I was used to with men I'd known for more of my life than I hadn't, but a new home. A new family. "Everybody take a seat and we can talk about the opening and the future."

"Sounds like a science fiction porno," Cruz snickered.

I ignored him and the little snickers that came from around the table. "Saint is the manager of The Barn Door so most things will go through him, including hiring. He's more than up for the job but don't give him any unnecessary shit." I kept my gaze on Saint so he knew I meant what I said.

"So pretty boy's in charge. I can deal with that." Slayer managed to pull a smile from the nervous man.

"Ford is on security. You met him earlier in the week. He's a little too green to join us down here right now, but soon. In the meantime, he's in charge of security." He might be a great prospect someday, but we needed to do everything in the right order. "The rest of you are on overall security for the opening tonight. That means keep an eye on the staff, like bartenders and waitresses. Make sure everything is consensual. We don't need any fucking trouble." Especially tonight.

Slayer raised his hand and I arched a brow at him. "Can we partake?"

"Fair question. Have fun." I didn't expect them to be saints, not with so much fucking and so much kink going on around them. "But, if it gets to be too much, there will be a lot of people, sex, kink, drinks, etcetera, then tell Saint and go get some fresh air. Right away.

And I'm sure it doesn't need to be said, but not when you're on the clock."

"Got it." Holden gave a short nod when my gaze landed on him and every man followed suit.

"Good. Now one final thing. Anything that happens in the club, stays in the fucking club. Not the MC and not the house. None of it. Got it?"

There was a long, pregnant pause before they all agreed and we filed out of the room. Giving the club one final walkthrough, I made my way back to the main house to have lunch with Maisie. Since I wouldn't be around for dinner, I promised her we'd eat lunch together.

The noise coming from the kitchen was much louder than usual, so I wasn't too surprised when I found Maisie and Peaches singing while they pranced around the kitchen. "Where's Martha?"

Both bodies stopped and turned to face me. "She was having trouble breathing, and I managed to convince Ditzy and Dum-Dum to take her to the doctor.

Maze and I are taking care of each other and lunch, aren't we chica?"

I narrowed my eyes. Last think I wanted was to have something wrong with the woman who made everything work around here and was like a second mother to all of us. "She going to be okay?"

"I think so. She said it was the heat and she just needed a nap, but I insisted she get checked out."

"You keep me informed," I said and turned to my little sister. Maisie's dark pigtails flopped all around as she lifted her arms for me to pick her up. "We made food. You hungry, Gunny?"

"I'm starved, honey."

"Good because we made chili and I got to shave the carrots. I got to mix the cornbread with my hands and lick the brownie spoon." She smacked her hands over her mouth and sent a wide-eyed stare at Peaches. "Oops."

"That's okay, you can't keep a secret. We're having brownies, and I let Maisie lick the spoon. Problem?"

Clearly she expected there to be a problem so I frowned, to give her what she wanted.

"Yeah there's a problem." I turned to Maisie who looked worried. "You didn't save me any of that spoon?"

"Nope. It was yummy too!" I tickled her until her whole body shook with laughter.

"It smells great in here. You cooked all this?"

Peaches nodded but she never turned to look at me and I was grateful, because the sight of her in a blue jean skirt with the little fringe at the hem was doing things it shouldn't to my body. It wasn't just those legs that I knew every inch of, it was the checkered shirt she wore and the way she'd tamed her curls into braids that poked out from the cowboy hat she wore proudly. I wondered if I could get her to ride me while she wore that hat and then my mind was there, watching her writhe under me and over me, in nothing but that hat. "Eyes up here, cowboy."

Dammit, she was standing less than a foot in front of me, mouthwatering tits right there. "I was making my way up, sweetheart."

Heat flared in her eyes but she shook it off with a shake of her head. "See something you like?"

Fuck yeah, I did. "Maybe."

"Doesn't Peaches look pretty? Like a real cowgirl!" With those curves she looked more like a fantasy, but it wasn't smart to disagree with little girls.

"She does," I agreed and set Maisie in the chair to my right while Peaches went back to the stove. "Do you ride, Peaches?"

She turned and put the food on the table as her lips twitched with humor. "On occasion, but only when the mood strikes."

Damn, I hoped the mood struck her soon because I was starving for her. It was supposed to be a one and done but fuck me if my body didn't crave hers. I wanted to fuck that tight pussy again, taste her sweet juices and watch the way she gave everything up in the name of passion. It was a total mind fuck, being with her, but like a fool I couldn't wait for another. "Does the mood strike often?"

"Enough," she said simply and took the seat beside Maisie to help her, something that rarely occurred to me. It hurt to admit it but watching Peaches teach my sister how to blow on her chili until it was cool enough to eat was domestic. Maternal. Two things I didn't want associated with the woman who had me rock hard under the table.

Chapter Sixteen

Peaches

One of the things I didn't miss about being surrounded by people was all the unspoken communication that went on. If it wasn't some low simmering sexual attraction, I preferred to be straight up about how I felt. That was, if I was inclined to share my feelings with anyone. Ever. But ever since lunch I'd felt on edge, off kilter and more than a little bit anxious. It was all Gunnar's fault.

His blue gaze had left a trail of heat down my left side and I'd just been helping Maisie eat the chili without burning her mouth.

He'd acted like I was trying to make her join a cult or something, staring a damn hole in the side of my head and every time I looked up, his face held an expression I couldn't figure out. It wasn't blank, there was too much intensity for blankness, but it wasn't overtly anything and that had left me feeling the way I had in damn near every foster home I'd been in.

Like a burden. Someone I wasn't pulling my weight. Like there was something I should have done but didn't do, and no one ever told me what it was. And then they never failed to let their disappointment show. I fucking hated that feeling more than I hated fear or vulnerability.

Just to get away from his intense gaze, I rushed through my own lunch and did the dishes quickly so I could spend some time outdoors. On my own. Far, far away from Gunnar Nilsson.

Actually, it wasn't that far. I walked around the ranch until I came upon a small manmade lake that actually had fish in it. They were small, bluish and silver, zipping through the water without a care in the world. Lucky fish. Lately, it seemed that all I had were cares and worries. For me and the people around me. It was exhausting. And that only made me worry even more.

Even Gunnar's incredible orgasms only helped for so long. I couldn't keep drinking from that well or else I might start having thoughts a girl like me shouldn't.

There was a sound in the distance, a disturbance of the leaves and twigs and rocks that peppered the grounds out this far. I froze, suddenly realizing why it was such a stupid fucking idea to come all the way out here. Alone. No one knew where I was. My shoes sat about ten feet to my left, a pair of cowboy boots I couldn't resist buying when I caught a glimpse of the turquoise stones embedded in them. Now I couldn't get to them without making my presence known. As it was, a big boulder shielded me from view but only if the sound came from behind me and that was hard to determine with so much quiet around.

"Fucking country life," I whisper-grumbled to myself, slowly slinking down the rock until I was on the ground and my toes danced with the edge of the water. A body broke through the crop of trees but his face was still shrouded in shadow. I held my breath and waited to see the figure raise a gun or speak into a covert comms device but neither happened.

"Peaches, you can't hide out forever."

"Cruz," I called out. "Fuck! What are you doing out here lurking in the woods?"

He blinked and scanned the area until our gazes collided and a smile split his face. "Checking on you. You've been gone a while."

"Didn't realize I was on a schedule." My time was my own. Just because I was staying here for a while didn't mean they could keep tabs on me. And that pissed me off.

"I know how you women are, and you've only got a few hours to get ready for the opening."

Tonight was the Grand Opening for The Barn Door, Gunnar's adult playground that if I was being honest, kind of got me a little hot and bothered. But only a little.

"I'm not going. It's hard enough to be a woman at a regular club. At your sex place, I'll never have a moment of peace. And Maisie is starting preschool in the morning. I want to be with her tonight."

My one and only visit to a sex club involved spending too much time saying, "no thanks" and not enough time screaming, "God, yes."

Cruz sighed and put his hands on his hips, his hair gleaming in the last shards of sunlight. When he smiled and the sun hit his beard, I couldn't help but smile. "You know we all need to be there tonight, which means it's the best place for you to be so we can all keep an eye on you."

"Like I told Gunnar, a casual eye is all right. I don't want any of you changing up your routines for me. If you see something, say something and we're all good." Even though the fear hadn't worn off that Cruz could have been someone else, I couldn't let these men disrupt their lives for me. I wouldn't.

"You don't have to worry about the guys hitting on you, you know?" He laughed at my affronted look. "You're hot as fuck and you know it, but we all know you're Gunnar's woman."

"No, I am not," I practically hissed the words at him.

Cruz just laughed again, the bastard, and held his hands up in a defensive gesture. "Whatever you say, babe. I'll swing by the main house around nine to pick you up. Don't forget to dress sexy, this ain't no church social."

He turned and walked away but it was slow enough that I never lost sight of him, not even after stopping to slip my boots back on, before I followed him back to the heart of the ranch. The big white house came into view with the large wraparound porch, complete with a wooden glider covered in flannel on the front porch. Martha's touches were everywhere with potted flowers on either side of the steps and wildflowers growing around the perimeter of the house. It was a great home. Gunnar had managed to give his sister something he'd never had, and I admired him for that. Dammit.

I sighed with reluctance. I needed to go to this grand opening tonight. I'd bought a sexy little outfit last week when I thought it might've been fun to go, but even though I knew I needed to go, I couldn't muster up a fuck about going.

Still, I indulged in a long hot bath making sure every inch of me was smooth, tidy, and smelling of perfume. Since it would be a shame to let the outfit go to waste, I took my time dressing, making sure I looked like the sexy, confident woman I wanted the world to see. A woman no one dared fuck with.

When I was properly glossed, smoothed, and smelling irresistible, I slipped into the sapphire blue teddy with the scalloped edges and a plunging neckline that would draw all kinds of attention to my D cups. The open panel in the back and the thong bottom would keep eyes on me, but the shimmery lace cape would let me decide how much they got to see. I grabbed a pair of black stilettos with ankle cuffs that matched the leather & lace cuffs on my wrists.

"There we go." I looked sexy and sassy and confident, but just innocent enough to make even the shy guys feel bold.

As I stood staring at myself in the mirror, I smiled. Not because I looked that good, though I did, but because I had a plan. I couldn't keep fucking Gunnar without messy emotions getting involved, but that didn't mean celibacy. The club was the perfect place for me tonight. Maybe a threesome would get those intense blue eyes out of mind, hell maybe a devil's threesome would make me forget how well his cock filled me up. Then again, maybe some girl on girl action would remind me that men were nothing but trouble. Whatever I found tonight, I would be open to it.

Except Gunnar. These thighs were closed for him. Permanently.

I let out a long breath and squared my shoulders. I was ready.

To have some kinky, Gunnar-free fun.

Chapter Seventeen

Gunnar

I couldn't believe I was actually nervous about tonight. Me and the guys got to The Barn Door an hour before opening to do a final run through and everything was perfect, yet I was still nervous. Me, Gunnar fucking Nilsson, nervous. I knew part of it was because this was the first thing I'd done on my own, without Cross and the guys, in more than a damn decade.

Yet here I was, doing it. Not on my own though, the guys from Hardtail Ranch had pitched in, taking on tasks without being asked. Like a real family. When the time came, the Opey Chapter of the Reckless Bastards would be damn near as good as the first. At least that was what it felt like tonight.

Everything was set for a night of success. Martha and the twins had Maisie. The DJ was already set up and music blared through strategically placed speakers that made the whole place pulse with heat and desire.

Two bartenders manned every bar and they would take turns delivering drinks and making sure everyone had what they needed. Within reason. Ford had the door covered, and I knew I wouldn't have to worry about that.

"Yo! Gunnar." Slayer strolled up with his lazy long-legged gait, long brown hair swinging behind him and a big ass grin on his face. "The bartender up front is looking pretty green and maybe a little scared of her own shadow."

Shit. She was an experienced bartender which is why I didn't say shit when Joplin hired her, but I needed to be sure she wouldn't run screaming halfway through the night. "Thanks Slayer. You seen Peaches?"

She was supposed to be here for opening night because it was the best place to make sure she was safe.

"Nah, but you know how women are. They always take forever to get ready for everything." He rolled his eyes and walked away. I turned and headed toward the front bar.

"Hey Jasmine, how's it going?"

Dark brown eyes looked up at me, and I understood exactly what Slayer meant about her being afraid of her own damn shadow. "Oh, hey Gunnar. Good. Just getting ready for the night."

"You gonna be okay with this?" She nodded and looked around, making me wonder if she was afraid of me or the club. "If you feel uncomfortable just say so. We have people here that will keep you safe from any unwanted attention, all right?"

Finally a small smile touched her pouty mouth. "Yeah. I'm good. Thanks for making sure though." She gave me another look and went back to work.

Another fire put out and I was feeling good but just to be safe I decided to do one final check of the rooms downstairs. All the equipment was brand new and shiny as fuck, even the low black and red lights of the private rooms. The leather gleamed, the silver sparkled and everything encouraged the members to indulge in their darkest, kinkiest desires.

I made my way to the back bar on the front level and nearly ran into Saint. "The line is already wrapped around the building. I think all the members have showed up."

Saint's expression was serious, as it always was but tonight his gaze was a little steadier and a little more direct. A smile crossed my face as the words sank in.

"Fuck yeah!" I held a fist up and though it took a second, he finally fist-bumped it with a smile.

"I'd better go and start greeting our members."

I clapped him on the back and smiled. "I'll go with ya." This was a big damn night for me and it was off to the best possible start. The only problem was Peaches. Where the hell was she? "You seen Peaches?"

He just shook his head and continued forward and as we approached the front door, I pushed thoughts of Peaches out of my mind and greeted The Barn Door members as Ford checked them in. The doors opened and slowly the club began to fill with members dressed in suits and slinky dresses, and others dressed in a lot less than that. Ninety minutes after opening the place was hot and the pulsing beat infused the air with a mixture of sex, desire, and adventure.

Bodies moved all around, on the dance floor couples and triples bumped and ground on one another, some just swayed slowly and kissed while their hands roamed and caressed. The booths were filled with people getting up close and personal with each other, talking about things like limits and desires while others didn't bother with a pretense.

At one table a woman knelt underneath, her hands stroking a man's thighs as she sucked him off. At the table he had a tit in his mouth and his hand between another woman's legs. The sight made me smile. And it made my dick stand up and take notice because this was exactly what I pictured for the place.

Thoughts of my hard dick brought to mind a curvy wild-haired woman who should be here by now. And wasn't. "Cruz, have you seen Peaches?"

He smiled and nodded. "You haven't? Oh man, she's around here somewhere." The gleam in his eyes put me on alert.

"Gettin' into trouble?"

Cruz shrugged, but even in the dark lights of the club I could see amusement and mischief in those eyes of his.

"Depends on what you mean by trouble." He must've seen the frustration on my face because he flashed a sympathetic smile. "She's in the VIP booth like you said."

I was on my feet without a word of thanks or acknowledgment but luckily Cruz was laid back as fuck, not letting much get to him. It was a quality I appreciated in those around me, but my focus was on finding Peaches and making sure she was safe. And steered clear of trouble.

The VIP tables were available by reservation only. The high backs and circular shape were meant for privacy and they had dedicated bottle service so the tables were only disturbed if they wanted to be. I found Peaches at the reserved table.

She wasn't alone. A man in an expensive suit and cowboy boots sat with her, whispering in her ear, maybe even brushing his lips across her neck if the closed-eye smile was any indication. For some reason it pissed me off even though I knew it shouldn't.

Yeah, we'd fucked a couple times, but I had no claims on her. That didn't stop the anger from coursing through me or the desire to rip that motherfucker apart from settling over me like a warm, welcoming woman. I took two steps toward the table when I felt a hand on my shoulder.

"Don't do it, man." Slayer stood at my side with a serious expression on his face. "I know what you're thinking but trust me if you go over there half-cocked that spitfire will do what you're thinking of, and worse, just to spite you. To prove she can."

My shoulders fell because, dammit, he was right. "Thanks, man."

"No problem." He flashed a smile and blended back into the crowd.

I took another glance over my shoulder at Peaches, who was laughing again but at least there was some distance between her and cowboy boots. Spotting one of our platinum members, Mayor Hal and his wife Lorna, I went to make sure they were having a good time. "Hal. Lorna. I trust you're enjoying yourselves?"

Lorna's green gaze gave me a thorough once over, and I knew exactly what was on her mind. "We are. This place is lovely." Her words came out like a purr and her tits were barely contained in the silk nightie she wore that skimmed the tops of her thighs. Lorna was a beautiful woman, but she tried too hard.

"Thanks. Have you had a chance to explore our specialty rooms downstairs?"

Hal's smile widened. "Headed there soon, I think." He flashed a hungry look at his wife, and I knew what was on his mind.

"Maybe you'll stop in and play with us later?" The way she was eye fucking me made her desire clear, but Mayor Hal was one man I couldn't afford to piss off. I needed to keep that man in my pocket.

"As incredible as that offer is, I only play when I'm not on the clock sweetheart. How about some of our best bourbon to loosen you guys up?" I motioned for one of the servers who quickly came and took care of the mayor and his wife.

I waited as long as I could, but Peaches was like a goddamn magnetic field, pulling me in, and I found myself standing in front of the VIP table where once again, she was not alone. This time a stacked blonde sat beside her with a hand on her thigh and her lips brushing soft, teasing kisses along the smooth honey brown skin of Peaches' shoulder. The blonde's free hand traced the sapphire lace that stretched over mouthwatering cleavage, tempting Peaches with soft touches.

"Ladies." They didn't move apart right away, but eventually Peaches opened her eyes and a small smile touched those plump lips.

"Gunnar." That was it, just my name with no emotion. Hell, I probably deserved it, but I didn't like it, not when she was looking hot as fuck in that outfit.

Before I could say another word or scare off the handsy blonde, a man in leather pants and more fucking cowboy boots approached.

"You said martinis so I asked for 'em extra dirty." He looked at me and smiled. "You joining us? I got a feeling these two will be a handful."

There was no fucking way Peaches or I were going anywhere with this guy. Peaches quirked a brow at me, challenging me to do what every fiber of my being was urging me to do. *Fuck it.* I stepped a little closer to the table and grabbed Peaches by the arm, pulling her to her feet and yanking her away from dirty martini and his handsy girlfriend.

"Get your paws off me, asshole!" Peaches continued to swat and smack at my hand and my arms. "Gunnar, seriously."

She could fight me all she wanted, but I was bigger and stronger, and determined. Determined to do what? I had no fucking clue, but the way my cock strained against my zipper was a big fucking hint. I couldn't take her to any of the rooms because they were all probably full of naked bodies doing dirty things to each other, which is exactly what I wanted—no *needed*—to do to Peaches.

"In," I told her when we came to stop in the dimly lit hall where my office was located right beside Joplin's.

Arms crossed and chin tilted up in defiance, Peaches scowled at me. "Fuck you, Gunnar. A couple of fucks doesn't give you the right to go all Neanderthal on me."

I placed my hand on her lower back and gave her a gentle push inside before kicking the door shut. "You shouldn't be offering it up to everyone at the club." I knew it was the wrong damn thing to say as soon as the words left my mouth, but the outraged look she shot me told me it was worse.

"You didn't mind when I offered it to you." Arms folded so her tits sat right on top of her arms, Peaches looked like a wet fucking dream in blue lace that only covered the good parts and even then, it was just barely. I ate up the sight of her smooth brown skin on display, the little bodysuit she wore clung to her curves. "Oh my God, you're jealous."

"Don't flatter yourself." The words came out before I had a chance to stop them and they sounded harsh. Too harsh.

"Good," she said, not even flinching at my words even though I could see a glimmer of hurt in her big brown eyes, lined with black and green liner that gave her sexy bedroom eyes. "Then you can let me get back to my night and stop acting like a protective older brother." She shoulder-checked me as she tried to exit and my hand automatically reached for her.

"I can't do that," I told her in a moment of honesty.

"Try."

She was right, I was acting like a possessive asshole and that was something I never did. But even as my brain screamed at my hand to release her, I stepped closer and put the other hand on her hip, letting my fingertips brush over the soft skin there. She licked her lips and that was all it took for my mouth to crash down on hers and claim her like I wanted to do ever since I saw that asshole in the cowboy boots with his hands all over her. Instead of refusing me and telling me where to take my shitty behavior, Peaches' hands went to my head and her fingertips kneaded my skull before she tugged my hair and brought me closer.

"Fuck you taste good," I told her and when she smiled, I attacked her mouth once again.

She moaned and let her hands slide down my neck and over my shoulders until both hands slid down my pecs and abs before coming to a rest at my waistband. My cock grew harder as her hands reached around and grabbed my ass, pulling me closer like she couldn't get enough either.

That thought fired up my desire for this woman, and when she hooked a leg over my hip so I could feel the scorching heat of her pussy, I lost control, pushing her up against the wall and lifting her in my arms.

"Gunnar," she moaned as I kissed and nibbled my way down her neck and across her collarbone. I let my tongue taste the smooth skin of her cleavage.

"I can feel how much you want me, Peaches." Her pussy was hot and wet and hungry for me.

"Then do something about it," she taunted, grinding against me.

That was just what I did, finding a nipple beneath the dark blue fabric. I pulled it into my mouth, sucking hard and scraping it with my teeth until she moaned. She tossed her head back with a smile of complete pleasure.

"Yes," she moaned, her anger all but forgotten as my hand slid between her thighs and found her pussy wet through her lingerie. "Don't. Tease."

A low laugh escaped at her bossy words, but I wanted to tease her, needed to do it for the way she teased me in that outfit. So I brushed a knuckle over her swollen pussy lips to make her gasp. "But teasing you is so fucking fun, Peaches."

A low growl escaped from deep in her gut. Before she could curse me again, I moved the blue fabric to the side and slid a finger into all that creamy goodness.

"Fuck," she moaned.

That one word came out on a sexy rasp and her head fell back against the wall, her pussy clenching tight around my finger.

"Gunnar, yes."

She was hot and wet, pulsing around my fingers because she was already close to orgasm. Changing up my grip so I could rub my thumb over her clit seemed to do the trick because she squeaked and put her trust in me, letting go and grinding against my hand as she chased her pleasure. She was so fucking beautiful in that deep blue with her mouth open as harsh breaths flew out of her.

"Come for me, Peaches. Right now."

She flashed me a look that said, *really* and I took her nipple again, pulling hard until her pussy squeezed so tight it nearly broke my finger. I didn't give a damn, not when the force of her orgasm nearly knocked me out and not when her pleasure flooded my hands.

"Gunnar, yes."

She was still coming, still clawing at my body like she didn't know whether to push me away or pull me closer. She made up her mind quick as her hands flew to my waistband and made quick fucking work of my belt, zipper and button while I undid the snaps on her teddy.

"Hurry," I said, breathing hard now. "So you don't mind the Neanderthal?"

I smiled and she smiled back, reaching between us to stroke my cock the moment is was free.

"Not when he's making me come and about to give me this dick."

As she spoke, she kept stroking, bring the slobbering tip of my cock closer and closer to where she was wet for me. A few drops of her juices spilled onto my cock and my control snapped.

I gave Peaches what she wanted, sliding my dick deep in one smooth stroke. She let out a satisfied sigh that matched mine and I stilled for a moment, enjoying the feel of her tight, hot walls pulsing around me.

"Gunnar," she moaned and dug her heels into my ass at the same time her hips began to roll.

"Yeah?" I flashed a grin even though my cock screamed at me to get moving, to give him some friction that we both wanted and needed.

"You gonna fuck me or set up camp?"

Her words made my whole body shake with laughter, something I never did when I was buried deep inside a woman. But she pulsed around me again in warning and my dick agreed that it was time to stop fucking around and just start fucking. I pulled all the way out with my hands gripping her ass tight, then slammed into her wet cunt over and over, pounding hard while she cried out her pleasure and clung to me.

She felt so fucking good I didn't want to stop. Not that I could have even if I'd wanted to because my body was on a mission of its own to explore the deepest parts of her until she was slick with sweat and begging me for another orgasm.

"Gunnar, please."

That was all it took, one little whispered plea and I was like putty, thrusting hard and deep, as fast as I could until the sound of our bodies smacking together overtook the thumping pulse of the music all around us. I grunted as my hips moved against hers, loving the way she bucked against me despite my grip on her.

"Oh, fuck." Her pussy was getting tighter and tighter, pulsing like it was trying to suck me dry.

And then her orgasm snuck up on her, sharp and powerful enough to make her whole body tremble as she rode it out.

"Fuck! Yes! There it is! Don't stop!" Waves upon waves of pleasure rolled over her even as I fucked her harder and harder, chasing down my own pleasure.

"Take it," she ordered as she held a beautiful bare tit up to my mouth, nipple hard enough to cut glass.

I paused half a beat and sucked that nipple into my mouth, rolling the hard tip around between my teeth while my cock plunged in and out of her, faster and faster. Another flutter started deep inside Peaches and knowing that I was about to make her come again did something dark and twisted to me. I gripped her harder, pressing my body as close to hers as I could while I fucked her like my life depended on it. Then she screamed my name as her body twitched with orgasm, the force of her pleasure yanking my own orgasm from me. "Ah, Peaches, fuck!"

My body was on fire, my lungs burned as sweat dripped down my face and chest and back, even as Peaches let her hands slip through the damp skin.

"Now that's some good dick."

I chuckled and stepped back until her feet hit the ground. Her legs shook a little as she tried to right her lingerie but Peaches never reached out to me for assistance.

"Thanks." I couldn't look away from her or those wild curls that gave her a deceptively angelic appearance despite those sinful curves and that dirty fucking mouth of hers. I wanted her again and I'd just had her and that pissed me off.

Something in her brown eyes shifted, as if she knew what I was thinking and she turned away from me, giving me the moment I needed to put my own clothes right and to put some much needed fucking distance between us.

Chapter Eighteen

Peaches

"Lick her pussy."

An incredibly buff and beautiful cocoa skinned man growled the order at the gorgeous Asian chick he was fucking doggy style and she obeyed right away, moving closer to the wide open legs capped off with a red landing strip. I gave her kudos for not going totally bare, happy to see I wasn't the only adult around who still had a hint of pubes. The scene on the other side of the glass was hot enough that I felt the wetness sticking to my thighs as the Asian chick closed her eyes and licked that girl's pussy like a pro. The guy gripped her tight, the same way Gunnar had done to me not even an hour ago, plowing into her in long hard strokes.

Inside the room, about a dozen men and women had gathered to watch, some of them getting so turned on that fingers and hands and mouths all sought human flesh of some kind, and I was half tempted to join them.

Not because I had some secret gang bang fantasy, though I wasn't completely opposed, but out of pure fucking spite that Gunnar, that blue eyed motherfucker, had fucked me and then left me alone in his office while his come dripped down my thigh. Not a fucking goodbye or a see you later or a thanks for the fuck.

Nothing.

It was a hot fuck, that much was for damn sure, but I'd had a hot threesome lined up and right now I could be that redhead getting her clit sucked like it was the fucking fountain of life. Instead, I was on the other side of the window sore and still horny as fuck. Thanks to that big dicked asshole, playing the role of a jealous Neanderthal when he had no fucking right.

Angry and disgusted, I left the viewing window before anyone's orgasm came crashing down, pussy still wet and pulsing. Hungry for more. A drink, that was what I needed, so I made my way upstairs, choosing the front bar instead of the back one where it sounded like a full blown orgy was going on.

"Beautiful, you have to let me buy you a drink." I looked up into light blue eyes with little threads of gold in them, a full smiling mouth and a thick head of wavy blond hair. He was gorgeous and looked to be about twenty-two years old, but the eight pack abs he was sporting had my nipples straining to get closer.

"I do, do I?"

He nodded. "If for no other reason than so I can enjoy looking at you without feeling like a creeper." His words made me laugh.

"Since you put it that way, I'll have a dirty martini." When the dark haired bartender stopped in front of us, I smiled at her. "Make it extra dirty, yeah?"

She nodded meekly and got busy making the drink, making me wonder what her story was, but I had enough since to know this was not the time or the venue to get to know her. Or anyone for that matter.

"You have a name, beautiful?"

"I do," I purred in his ear but suddenly I felt uneasy, not because of him exactly but because he was a stranger. I couldn't tell him my real name, not when there were professional assassins out there looking to fill my body with bullets. So I settled on a name he would believe. "Sasha."

"Damn, is that sexy!" His Texas twang was thick, and he was a big corn fed boy who looked eager to please, which suited me just fine for the moment.

"Thanks. What about you?"

"Dean." He raised his glass with a smile. "To beautiful women with sexy names and the lucky bastards who find them."

"Cheers," I said toasting him with my drink.

Dean wasn't a dazzling conversationalist but he was good looking and charming, just what I needed. He was also on the prowl and made no secret about it as his thumb stroked my knee up to my thigh, and all I could think about was Gunnar's come still inside me.

"Naughty boy."

He flashed a good ol' boy smile that only made him more appealing and did it again. "I'm tryin' to be. Want to join me, Sasha?"

Hell yes I wanted to join him. And if I was even the slightest bit bothered by the fact that Gunnar's scent still lingered on my skin, I pushed it away and took a long unladylike gulp of my martini. It was dirty like me and I didn't give shit, being ladylike was totally fucking overrated.

"Absolutely." I could do this. I would because I could.

A throat cleared behind Dean and we both turned to look and found Gunnar.

"Fuck off," he barked at Dean, who must've realized that this wasn't a fight he could win. He flashed a regretful smile and sauntered off. Too bad, because he was hot as fuck.

"What the fuck, Peaches?"

I stared at him, laughing to myself at his nerve. "What the fuck *what*, Gunnar? I'm just doing what we're doing. We fucked, and you left so I'm moving on. I'm in a goddamn sex club! That's what we do, isn't it? No big deal. Right?"

He was angry enough that I swear, flames shot out of ears as he glared at me.

"I'm working," he snarled.

"And I'm not. I finished my work days ago. I'm here because I was guilted into coming and somehow, I planned to have fun until some fucking caveman got jealous. You got what you wanted Gunny, so go away, unless scaring away paying members is part of your business plan?"

"Such a smart fucking mouth," he growled. I smiled, leaning my head to the side.

"Thank you." He stepped close enough that I could see the different shades of blue in his eyes.

"It wasn't a compliment."

I shrugged. "It felt like one to me. Now if you'll excuse me, I think Dean—"

The rest of that sentence was put to an immediate halt by the force of our mouths colliding right there in front of the bar. His tongue moved masterfully against my own and his hands sculpted over my tits, my hips and my ass where his hands settled in a tight grip. Gunnar ripped his mouth from mine and sucked in several deep breaths.

"You talk too fucking much."

He was probably right and I wasn't all that bothered by his statement, but my body was very hot and super fucking bothered. I grabbed his arm and tugged him through the crowd of mostly naked gyrating bodies until we were back in his small, dimly lit office.

"I'm okay with that."

His chuckle was deep and masculine, and I watched the play of muscles under his t-shirt when he turned to close and lock his office door.

"You, Peaches, are fucking with my concentration."

"That sounds like a *you* problem, not a *me* problem."

He frowned and I pushed myself up onto his desk and spread my legs wide until his gaze settled right where I wanted it.

"Now do you want to argue or do you want to have some fun so you can walk away again?"

My hand went between my legs, where I was embarrassingly wet but not enough to care, not when his sexy ass self was staring at my pussy like it was a birthday cake with his name on it.

"Fuck me, I wish I could resist you."

That low guttural growl hit me right between my thighs, sending even more wetness to flood my cunt. Gunnar saw it too, taking two fingers and rubbing the moisture all over my pussy through the fabric of my teddy. "At least I know you want me just as bad."

I did. No matter how stupid it was, I wanted him. Bad. "Never said I didn't." When he caught sight of the snaps on my crotch, he opened them with nothing more than a flick of his fingers.

"So fucking wet already," he growled and stepped between my legs.

I licked my lips at the sight of him, staring at me like I was the beginning and end of all his sexual fantasies. "What are you gonna do about it?"

In response, he slipped his middle finger deep into me and twisted, causing tingles to run up and down my spine until I arched into his touch.

"That's a good start but I think you need to learn not to talk so much."

I laughed and tossed my head back. "A lesson you'd do well to learn when there's a hot woman with her pussy on display."

"Exactly right," he agreed as his hands went to his belt and then his jeans, freeing his cock as he walked around the desk and stopped behind me. "Lean back."

I did, more out of curiosity than any sense of obedience because let's face it, whatever he had in store, my slut of a body wanted it. Bad. Gunnar was upside down in this position but his blue eyes never left my body, heavy like a caress as he took it all in. "Now what?"

"You know what." He was right. That long thick erection was less than an inch away and my mouth watered to see if it was as good as it tasted. When he stroked his cock and a few beads of cream appeared at the tip, I grabbed him and pulled him to me, swiping my tongue across the slit.

"Fuck, that's right, Peaches. Take this cock."

I didn't give a damn what it said about me that his words had my pussy flooding like the Mississippi River because I was in control. His cock was in my hands and my mouth and Gunnar was at my mercy. Mine. I took more of him into my mouth and closed my eyes so there was only the scent of him and the sound of him to guide me.

"Oh fuck, Peaches." He took a step closer and thrust his hips until his cock slid down my throat, nearly choking me. It took a minute to adjust but I was more than up for the task, even when he began to fuck my mouth a little rough and a whole lot of dirty.

"Fuck," he growled when my tongue swiped his balls.

I smiled but my mouth never stopped working his dick because the sounds he made, the way his thighs trembled turned me on in a way that even shocked me. Then he leaned closer, sending his cock deeper down my throat, but a second later, his cool tongue and soft lips were between my legs making me squirm.

His tongue moved over my clit, flicking and sucking. I writhed against him while he fucked my mouth. I moaned around him and Gunnar shivered, spreading me wider and licked me until I bucked off the table and felt the juices of my orgasm slide down my ass.

"Oh fuck," I mumbled around his cock, but Gunnar didn't stop his own mouth. He sucked my clit and fucked my mouth for what felt like forever and that was when I felt it, his cock a little harder and little longer as his orgasm approached.

"Fuck," he growled against my clit, sending shockwaves through me as the orgasm started again. I swallowed around his cock and he lost it, sending long spurts of hot come down my throat, all the while his lips remained wrapped around my clit.

I was overheated and breathing was hard, but it was the single hottest orgasm of my life, and I couldn't bring myself to put a stop to it. Yet. My body felt good, damn good. Lazy and satisfied. I couldn't resist licking his cock one last time before it slipped from my mouth. "Oh fuck," I gasped when oxygen flooded my lungs all at once.

"Why can't I get enough of you?" His words weren't happy, they were annoyed. The bastard.

Whatever smartass retort was on my mouth remained unspoken as a knock sounded at the door. Good, because it was my turn to make a clean getaway.

Chapter Nineteen

Gunnar

I wanted to tell whoever it was on the other side of the door to go the fuck away but Peaches slipped away from me and out the door, giving Saint his opening. His gaze darted around the room, probably looking for evidence of another blowout between me and Peaches. When he found none, a small knowing smile touched his lips and that just pissed me off.

"What?" My tone was unnecessary but goddammit, Peaches had run away and evidence of her was all over my mouth and cock.

"We have a problem. The computer system flickered for a second or two, but it was still working. Until about five minutes ago."

"Shit. Why did you wait five minutes to tell me?" I was being an asshole, luckily Saint didn't call me out on it.

"Ford did everything Peaches told him to before realizing he couldn't handle it on his own. He came close a few times but it went completely black."

"Fuck!" It was the last goddamn thing I needed on tonight of all nights, when The Barn Door was filled with members looking to have a good time. At this establishment a good time meant free flowing drinks, toy and equipment rentals and for some, private rooms where they could act out their filthiest fantasies without a soul ever knowing. And the computer system made all of that happen. "Did you tell Peaches?"

He shook his head and ran a hand through his close cropped brown hair. "She looked like she was in a bit of a hurry, and I figured you'd want to know first."

He looked nervous but he was right, dammit.

This was my club, my business, and my ass on the line. Something I should have fucking remembered instead of fucking Peaches on my desk.

"Dammit," I spit out, pissed at myself. I needed to do better. To *be* better. What the fuck was I thinking, burying my dick into a woman I could barely stand when I should have been mingling with members and making sure everything ran smoothly? Especially tonight.

"Give me a minute and then I'll be right up."

"Sure thing."

"And Saint?"

He turned with a wary look in his dark green eyes. "Yeah?"

"Thanks. You're doing a great job tonight."

A small smile touched his lips. "Thanks, Boss. That means a lot." And then he was gone.

I slipped out of the office soon after and found one of the six private bathrooms to clean up in and make myself look like the owner of this goddamn establishment instead of one of its horny members. It wasn't helping to beat myself up about it, but I couldn't help but feel responsible for the system crashing. This was my shit, and it all was on me if it failed or succeeded.

This was my third shot, hell this was Maisie's shot at a real life, a normal life, and I was already fucking it up. After splashing some cool water on my face and then my hair, I felt almost normal. I made my way up to the security booth where Ford waited with a cautious smile.

"Hey, Boss. Joplin tell you the system is fucked?"

"Yep. What did you do?" He rattled off a bunch of fucking words that didn't mean a damn thing to me. "In English."

"I tried to reboot the system like Peaches suggested. It worked but only for a minute. I backed up the footage and deleted it from the computer to see if that helped and it did, but again only temporarily." He raked a hand through his blond hair and let out a long sigh. "I tried everything she said, even went through my notes and none of it's working."

A rock settled in my gut, wiping away nearly all traces of the pleasure I'd felt just a few minutes ago with Peaches' sweet thick lips wrapped around my cock. She was the last goddamn person I should've been thinking about, but the way she let me fuck her face and seeing how much it turned her on was something I wouldn't forget anytime soon.

"Should we find her?"

I blinked at Ford's words, realizing I'd all but tuned him out for the last few seconds. "What?"

"Peaches. Should we find her? If anyone can help with this shit storm, it's her."

He was right. The whole goddamn system was down, from the security footage, the ID scans, the point of sale systems, every fucking thing.

"Yeah," I said, trying to get my ass in gear. Ford frowned at my reluctant tone but wisely kept his mouth shut. Of course he thought it was strange I didn't want the person who'd installed the damn system to see why it wasn't working. That was the logical choice.

"I'll do it, you keep trying."

"Got it, Boss." He saluted me, and even though I hated it, I decided now wasn't the time to get on his ass about it. I had more important shit to worry about.

When I stepped back inside the main part of the club, I could see the members getting restless. The music still played, but the Bluetooth connecting the speakers was also fucked so only the front half of the club had a soundtrack. Shit, this was not good. Not at all. If I didn't get this fixed in the next few minutes, my opening night would turn to shit.

"Jasmine!" She looked up with wide, frightened eyes but quickly masked the emotions.

"Yeah?"

"Free drinks. Get 'em going around. Now." She nodded, put her head down and got to work. She might be terrified of me, but the girl had a serious work ethic and I respected the hell out of that. Scanning the room, there was no sign of Peaches and I tensed. Had she stopped in one of the rooms to get another fix?

Slayer stood at my side and looked out at all the people milling about. "Gunnar, the natives are getting' restless." A few of them didn't seem to mind that there was no music or no booze, because they had everything they wanted in their mouths already.

"We gotta find Peaches," I said. "Now."

"She's in the coat room."

Leaving. I could see the unspoken words in Slayer's eyes. Peaches was trying to get away from me. "Keep an eye on shit while I deal with this."

"No problem." His words were filled with amusement and I flipped him off as I walked away, which only made him laugh louder and harder. "Make sure you say please and thank you," he called out behind me, still laughing his ass off.

Chapter Twenty

Peaches

Somebody was getting it on the coat room. It was cliché as hell but still, it made me laugh. I hoped it was the sweet little coat check girl with the blonde pigtails because she looked like she needed a good hard fuck from the wrong man. I was happy for her, really, I was. But I needed my damn coat because there was no way in hell I'd walk outside in this teddy without a knife, brass knuckles, or a pipe.

That's right, I was running. Turning tail. Getting the fuck out of Dodge. My body hummed with pleasure and staying any longer would only put a damper on that, so I was cutting out early. Without regard to my safety.

But it sounded like the couple, or maybe thruple, in the coat room were nowhere near being finished, so I turned and went in search of another form of fortification. A cocktail.

"There you are." Gunnar's voice was gruff as usual and his face was twisted in irritation.

"Looking for me?" I didn't mean to sound so flirtatious but every time this man was near, my body wanted him no matter what the rest of me had to say about it.

"Yeah. I need you."

Despite my better judgment and my wise reminders earlier, a smile curved up the corners of my mouth. "That sounds promising," I purred.

Gunnar rolled his blue eyes to the sky, and I felt like a fucking idiot. He wasn't here for me or for more of my hot body.

"What do you need?" Because *of course*, he'd already fucked me twice today; he was done with me.

"The whole fucking system is down, and Ford has tried everything. Nothing is working. I need you to take a look at it."

A shock went through me as I realized the significance. I wanted to tell him to go fuck himself, but this was my system. And I was damn good at systems. My reputation was on the line if I didn't get it up and running. "Okay," I mumbled as I brushed past him, I ignored the way my nipples tightened to peaks and the low, hungry sensation in my belly.

"He's in the security booth."

"I know." I lengthened my strides to get away from Gunnar and because I wanted to solve this problem quickly and get the fuck to my room where I could be alone with my thoughts.

"What's up?" I asked Ford who'd been staring a hole into the computer screen.

"Not a goddamn thing is up, that's what."

Hearing him curse with that baby face felt wrong, but I wasn't in the mood to be playful, so I bumped him aside with my hip and sat down. Gunnar and Ford were right, the system was completely and totally down and there was no reason why.

At least not on the surface.

"What is it?" Ford asked.

I ignored his angry tone and just answered. "I'll let you know when I figure it out."

Even though I was pissed at Gunnar for not saying one damn word about what had happened between us, this was exactly the distraction I needed. Work was my favorite way to escape when life got too messy because code was straightforward even if it wasn't simple. With coding and computers, I knew what I was doing. I could figure out any problem. Unlike people, who I could know for a fucking lifetime and never figure them out.

"Shit," I said, sensing the issue, Gunnar hot on my heels.

"What is it? Tell me," Gunnar barked, and I glared up at him.

"Calm your tits." I turned to Ford. "Did you give anyone the Wi-Fi password?"

He blinked and shook his head. "No and I wouldn't. If I have to use my mobile data so does everyone else."

There was no hack or attempt to break into the system, so I knew there was nothing to worry about. A few minutes later, I found the problem and a few seconds after that, it was all fixed. "Problem solved."

"What was it? Did someone try to hack the system?"

"No. Someone used the club's Wi-Fi and downloaded something they shouldn't have. It's fixed and the password has been changed," I told him as I scribbled the new password on the nearest piece of paper before I handed it to Ford. "Make sure Gunnar and Joplin have it but *don't* send it by email."

He frowned. "So you want to me write it down for them?"

I smiled at his adorable little face and patted his cheek. "Exactly. Is that all?"

"It is from me," Ford said with a charmingly boyish smile. "Unless you want to buy me a drink?"

I laughed. "Are you even old enough to drink?"

Ford put a hand to his chest and staggered back. "You wound me, Peaches."

"I doubt that very much. Have a good night." I had to slide past Gunnar to leave the small room and as I did, I tried my damnedest not to touch him or get a whiff of his masculine scent.

I headed back to the coat room, hoping the coat check girl had gotten hers so I could get my coat and get the hell out of here. A hand wrapped around my arm and even though I knew who it was, I turned, ready to punch the fuck out of him. "What?"

"Whoa, what's your problem?"

"Don't sneak up on women in dark halls and grab them." It was a stretch but it was also good advice and I titled my chin defiantly when he arched a brow at me. "Did you want something, Gunnar?"

"Yeah." He was nervous, spearing his fingers through his hair a half dozen times before he spoke again. "I uhm, just wanted to talk to you for a minute."

His tone wasn't that of a man who wanted to drag me to the nearest dark corner and give me another orgasm, but I nodded for him to continue. "Okay."

"The sex was incredible. Amazing. Hot as fuck. But it was just sex and it can't happen again."

It was no fucking comfort at all that Gunnar looked like he didn't want to be saying the words coming out of his mouth, but he was saying them and even though I hated it, I felt hurt.

Angry.

Not good enough. And that was one emotion I promised I would never feel again so I nodded and took a step back.

"Okay."

"Don't be angry, Peaches. Believe me, you're a great fuck. But I can't do a relationship right now, not with the ranch and the club and Maisie, there's too much going on."

He reached out to me, and I stepped back out of his reach. "Did I ask you for a relationship, Gunnar? Did I even ask you for a repeat performance?"

"No, but—"

"But you think a few good fucks and I'm already picturing you with a white picket fence, don't you?" I shook my head, hurt and disgusted and pissed off that I felt any of those things where he was concerned. "Don't worry Gunnar, I got your message. Loud and clear."

With as much dignity as a girl could muster in a sapphire lace Teddy, I scooted past him and walked out of the club with my head held high, my emotions pushed deep down just in case someone stopped me before I reached my final destination for the evening.

Luckily no one did, and I was able to rinse off all traces of Gunnar and the night at The Barn Door before slipping into a pair of comfortable pajama pants and a plain tank top. I grabbed a bottle of Maker's Mark from the liquor cabinet in the living room and took it back upstairs to the balcony connected to my room.

I sat out there for hours trying to figure out why I felt anything about Gunnar's words. He was an asshole, had been from the second I'd met him. He hadn't treated my girl Vivi like she was worth anything, and he'd treated me even worse, but I fucked him. Worse, I *let* him fuck me. More than once. And yet, I was the fool who wanted to do it again and again. What the hell was wrong with me?

I had no fucking clue but I had a bottle of bourbon to help me figure it all out.

Chapter Twenty-One

Gunnar

The morning after the opening I woke up early to a pot of coffee on despite the fact that Martha hadn't come in yet. As Peaches predicted, her trip to the doctor had been a false alarm. I'd offered her a few days off to rest but she'd refused, insisting she was back to normal.

It was too early even for the Bennett women to be at Hardtail Ranch, which gave me time to grab a big mug of coffee, probably made by Peaches, and head to the back porch early enough to watch the sun rise. It was enough to brighten my mood.

At least until I thought about the look in Peaches' big brown eyes when I told her she was nothing more than a good hard fuck. She wasn't devastated, but the hurt at my harsh words was pretty fucking hard to miss. And it wouldn't have been so bad if she'd screamed and told me what a worthless bastard I was.

But Peaches didn't do that. She'd notched her chin up and squared her shoulders before walking away. The strength she showed was impressive and as guilty as I felt, I knew it was the right thing.

I didn't have time for a woman, especially one like Peaches who brought trouble with her everywhere she went. Hell, even now she had assassins from the government and God knows who else after her. I had Maisie to think about not to mention getting the Opey Chapter up and running now that Cross had given us the go ahead. So yeah, there was too much to worry about to add a woman to the mix.

That didn't help me sleep last night. Even after all the drama at the club with the computers, the opening had gone even better than I'd expected.

"Gunny, whatcha doing?"

Maisie's quiet little girl voice pulled me from my thoughts and a smile instantly crossed my face. "I'm watching the sun rise, baby girl, what are you doing?"

"Looking for you. Miss Martha has a doctor's appointment, and I need to eat before school!" She darted back inside the house, letting the screen door smack against the frame loudly in her excitement. She was excited for her first day of preschool but after a long damn opening last night all I could think of was who in the hell started preschool on a Friday? Oh, right. Peaches had set up Maisie's preschool.

Her excitement meant the world to me, especially since it appeared that her sadness over our mother's death and leaving Mayhem had all but disappeared over the last few weeks, so I stood and took my empty coffee cup to the kitchen.

"Okay Squirt, what do you want to eat? We have cereal or oatmeal." I groaned at the options because that was no way to start the first day of preschool.

One look at Maisie's scrunched up face said she agreed. "What else?"

I laughed and sifted through the fridge until I found a few things that could work. "How about a BLT?"

Her smile spread slowly until her blue eyes practically disappeared, but the swinging of her lopsided ponytail made me smile right along with her.

"Yummy!" she squealed.

"Can you get dressed while I get breakfast going?" The bacon would have to go into the oven because whether she wanted it or not, Maisie needed help or else she'd end up wearing her funeral dress with a Superwoman t-shirt on top of it.

"Second thought, go brush your teeth and I'll be up in a minute."

"Miss Martha already laid out my clothes, Gunny, so I can do it. I'm a big girl now!" Before I could tell her to stick with washing her face and brushing her teeth, her little feet pounded up the stairs and into her room.

It felt good to see her growing more independent as the days passed, but dammit it made me realize how much time I was missing with her. Since we'd gotten to Texas, our time together had dwindled, with overseeing the club opening and helping the vets settle on the ranch. It was something I made a promise to myself to do as I assembled our BLT's, got Maisie dressed and fed just as Martha arrived with her demon spawn. "How are you feeling today Martha?"

She smiled and patted my cheek. "Good, thanks. Don't you worry about me Gunnar, I'll outlive you all."

Her words made me laugh, and I wrapped an arm around the older woman who'd become like an older aunt to me and a grandmother figure to my sister. "I don't doubt that for a minute, Miss Martha. In fact, I'm counting on it."

She pushed at my chest and bent down in time to catch Maisie's running hug. "Save that charm for the young women. Once you stop scowling at the world, they'll be lining up for a big strapping boy like you."

No one had called me a boy since the cop who'd caught me shoplifting when I was ten. "I'll take it under advisement."

Maisie stood between us, staring up with a nervous expression on her adorable little face, and I dropped down so we were eyeball to eyeball. "Hey kiddo, are you ready for your first day of school?"

She nodded, but she wasn't old enough or experienced enough to hide the wariness darkening eyes the same color as mine. "Yep, but what if I don't make any friends?"

"I don't think that's possible, but if that happens, we'll find a school where the kids aren't so stupid. Deal?"

She giggled and threw herself into my arms. "Deal! Miss Martha knows all my new teachers so she's taking me to school today."

"She does? Are you sure you don't want me to take you?"

"No, Gunny, I'm a big girl. Love you!"

"I love you too, Squirt. Now you better get going before you're late for school and get stuck next to the smelly kid." She giggled again and I squeezed her tighter, sending a prayer to whoever might be listening that they would give my kid sister the best first day of preschool a kid ever had. "Have a good day."

"You too," she shot back and smacked a kiss to my cheek before running off behind Martha.

"What's the big deal anyway, billions of kids start school every year."

Evelyn stood in the doorway between the living room and kitchen, arms crossed and wearing too much makeup—and heels—for a domestic worker.

I glared at her and took a step forward. "Don't you have work to do?"

Evelyn quickly realized that I wasn't fucking around because her arms fell to her sides, her expression held a hint of fear, and she got her scrawny ass to work. There was no fucking way in hell I'd make the trip to The Barn Door just to do paperwork when it could be done right here. There was about an hours' worth of emails to go through, everything from vendors looking to be paid, people inquiring about jobs on the ranch, my VA contact looking to send a few more vets my way and most surprising of all, there were three dozen new applications for The Barn Door membership. That lightened my mood more than anything else could have.

It meant last night had gone even better than expected.

"What's that smile for, Boss?" Saint appeared in the doorway with a small smile of his own, making me wonder if he'd gotten lucky last night.

I told him the good news and his smile brightened. "Did you need something, Saint?"

His brows dipped low in confusion. "You said to show up at ten so we could go over last night's receipts." He looked uncertain, and I took pity on the guy.

"You're right, I did. I forgot. Come on in," I gestured him inside and he closed the door without prompting before taking a seat.

"You've looked at them already?"

"I did and we did great, better than projected even. By a large margin." Even though I had my reservations about him, Joplin had proven to be an effective manager, his skittishness notwithstanding. "See for yourself," he said and produced a black flash drive from his pocket.

I took a few minutes to look over the spreadsheets and let out a low whistle. "When the hell did you have time to do all of this?" He'd tallied up the receipts for the night and even broke down how much came from the bars, the rooms, and the special equipment fees.

Saint shrugged, his eyes darting around the room, but the pink that covered his cheeks told me that my words pleased him. "I don't sleep much and I like to keep busy."

I knew the haunted look in his eyes. PTSD. I also knew that a man, especially a military man, had to come to the conclusion on his own before he could be helped.

"Talk to Wheeler's brother, Mitch, if you need to. Strict confidentiality and all that shit," I told him to take off some of the pressure.

To his credit, Saint didn't deny it or pretend not to know what the fuck I was talking about. "I don't know, talking about all this shit isn't my strong suit."

I laughed. "You're a man, of course it ain't. But if we're gonna be brothers, and I'm planning on that, then I need you to try."

He didn't look convinced and I didn't expect him to because admitting he needed help was damn hard. Even harder when he was already scarred and wary of strangers.

"Besides, talking about it sucks a fuck of a lot less than the nightmares."

Something like hope flashed in his eyes and he shrugged. "I'll think about it."

"That's all I can ask," I said.

Without another word on the subject, we went over the receipts and worked on putting together a calendar of events for The Barn Door. He had some good ideas and now that I knew the source of his strange behavior, I was able to overlook his quirks.

"I think that's enough for today," I said, pushing back from the computer.

He looked relieved and stood just as the phone rang. "I'll let you get that. Thanks for the talk, Gunnar."

I smiled and pulled my cell from the desk drawer. "Thanks for not calling me Boss again. Thought I was gonna have to kick your ass."

The phone stopped ringing and started again as Joplin left the office laughing. I didn't recognize the number, but I picked up anyway. "Yeah?"

"Mr. Nilsson?" The voice was feminine and unrecognizable, instantly putting me on alert.

I stood and turned to look at the window facing the bunk house. "Yeah, who is this?"

"Annie Miller. I'm Maisie's preschool teacher." She paused and my mind raced, thinking of all the reasons she could be calling.

"Is Maisie all right?"

Annie Miller sighed hesitantly. "Maisie has been vomiting and she has a mild fever. We have her in the nurse's station lying down, but she needs to go home."

Shit. "I'll be right there," I told her and ended the call abruptly. Maisie was sick. That in itself wasn't an unusual occurrence, but back in Mayhem I had all the Reckless Bastards and their old ladies on hand to help with things like sick kids. Here in Opey I was on my own, and I'd been shirking my responsibilities as her guardian.

My feet carried me to the kitchen where I was certain Martha would have the answers I needed, but the kitchen was empty. I found Adrian in the laundry room. "Where's Martha?"

Without looking my way, she answered. "Probably still in town doing the shopping. We're low on everything because of her health scare."

Right, dammit. "Thanks," I mumbled and left, knowing I would have to figure it out on my own. With my phone in hand, I scrolled through a few pages of local pediatricians, wondering if it made me a bad parent if I just closed my eyes and pointed to one. It wasn't the worst option, but as I grew closer to the barn where most of the vehicles were parked, I decided the ER was the best choice for now.

"Shit," I said when I saw the empty parking spot. My truck was gone and I remembered that Holden had taken it to go pick up some feed and other ranch essentials in town. I couldn't exactly pick up my four-year-old sister on the back of a motorcycle or the ATV I'd retrieved from Peaches campsite and most of the guys had taken off after a long night at The Barn Door.

Only one car remained, and I smiled because I had the keys to it.

At least I *did* have the keys, but after a few minutes of searching until I emptied all the drawers on my dresser, I realized that Peaches must have stolen them back. It could only mean one thing but my first priority was Maisie, so I pushed everything else from my mind and steeled myself for the argument to come.

Chapter Twenty-Two

Peaches

Maybe I was a coward for staying in my room all morning and well into the early afternoon, but I didn't give a damn. Sometimes a girl just needed some time to herself. Since I couldn't just leave and go back home, the small room worked well as a refuge. It killed me to stay in the confines of those four walls even as I heard Maisie's excited voice babbling about her first day of preschool. I wanted more than anything to have breakfast with her and listen to all her hopes and dreams for the start of her education.

But as adorable and lovable as she was, Maisie was not my family nor my responsibility. I had no rights to her, her time or her big moments in life. So I stayed where I was, under the blankets, and stared up at the cracks in the ceiling. Thinking about the shit show my life had become.

I was homeless, at the moment also jobless, and stranded. In Texas. It wasn't exactly what I had in mind for my future, but I wasn't the type of chick to throw a pity party for myself. I showered and dressed before retiring back to my room. Not to hide, though. Not that again. It was time to be proactive about all the shit that was happening *to* me so that I could get on with my life and leave Hardtail Ranch and its gruff, asshole owner, in my rearview mirror.

There had been no movement at my apartment for months, but that didn't give me any sense of relief. It only meant that they now knew I was no longer in New York.

"Well fuck." I knew what I had to do and picked up my phone.

"At least you got a new number," Vivi yawned into the phone.

"Why the hell are you yawning at noon? On second thought, don't tell me." Whatever kinky sexy fun she was having with Jag would only remind me of last night's humiliation.

Vivi groaned followed by sounds of her moving around. "No fun sex games, I'm afraid. Just an annoying baby zapping all of my energy so he or she can grow big and strong. The usual crap but that's not why you're calling."

"No." She knew me well so there was no point in lying. "Expect trouble to head your way soon if it hasn't gotten there already."

I told her all about the dead air where the men trying to kill me were concerned.

"I'm not dumb enough to think they've given up, and since you're my only connection I'm guessing Mayhem will be the next stop."

The other end of the line was silent. Vivi was thinking, running through about a million different scenarios. "The boys are on alert and expecting trouble, but so far none has showed up. How are things on the ranch?"

"The usual." There was no way in hell I would tell her about letting Gunnar fuck me six ways from Sunday before telling me I was nothing more than a good fuck. "Boring. Safe. Grumpy as fuck."

She chuckled and my heart ached, wishing I was with my best friend as she became a mother. "Right now, those are good things Peaches."

"So says you," I grumbled. "Any signs of trouble?"

"None that I know of and Jag hasn't said a word to me. Then again, he thinks the baby growing in my belly has turned me into spun glass, and he's doing his best to wrap me up in cotton."

My best friend *tried* to sound put out about Jag's behavior but I knew her too well.

"You love it. Admit it."

"A little. Maybe. And if you tell him that, I'll find a way to make the world think you're related to those fuckin' billionaire bitches on that new TV show." She laughed at her own threat and I groaned.

"If I'm lucky, the assassins will take one of them out by mistake and I can get on with my life." That was mean and macabre, but I was beyond being able to handle this all with a shrug and a smile.

"Is it that bad on the ranch?"

I sighed because no, it wasn't. "It's not the worst place I've been forced to lay my head, but it's still a place I *have* to be."

"Gunnar's treating you well?"

I suppressed a laugh. "He hasn't kicked me out yet, Vivi, so let's just call that progress." We caught up some more before she succumbed to some disgusting craving ending, the call and leaving me alone with my thoughts.

Again.

A knock sounded on the door and before I could think better of it, I opened the door, expecting one of Martha's asshole daughters. Instead it was *the* asshole himself.

"Yes?"

"You took the keys from my room."

"No, I reclaimed my keys that you stole. From me." If he thought a few orgasms would make me an obedient little fuck toy, he had another think coming.

"I need them," he barked at me and held out his hand, which I stared at blankly.

Gunnar groaned his frustration and raked a hand through his thick black hair that was growing longer every day.

"Maisie is sick. Martha is gone, and Holden has my truck." He said a few more words which I ignored in an effort to grab my keys and bag while stepping into a pair of sneakers.

Just because he was a dick didn't mean I would ever let Maisie suffer, not if I could help it. Gunnar stared at me suspiciously, a look that was becoming as familiar to me as my own damn reflection. I stepped around him and jogged down the steps, making my way to the makeshift car lot behind the barn.

"What the fuck, Peaches?" he said, jogging to keep up with me.

Sliding behind the steering wheel, I glared at him. "Are you coming or do you think the force of your anger will somehow get her back to the ranch?" Stubborn damn man.

Without a word, he slid into the passenger seat and pulled the seatbelt across his body. Arms folded, he stared straight ahead while I got us to the only school in Opey, a long red brick building that housed all the school-aged kids from preschool to high school.

"Stay here," he growled, not bothering to spare me a glance.

"Nah, I was thinking I'd go to the nearest mall and leave Maisie stranded."

His dark look intensified at my sarcasm. I looked away first, not in defeat but because Maisie was sick and waiting. "Well? They're not gonna bring her out for you, Gunnar."

Finally he was out of the car, stalking toward the building with all the grace of a big game cat. A big, angry but graceful panther, he even had the same slick hair and deep blue eyes. It was a quirk of fate that a guy like Gunnar could look so good yet was a world class asshole. Like nature had to even things out a bit.

While Gunnar was gone, I gave myself a mental pep talk. There would be no more snarky comments or sarcasm, because that made it seem like he mattered to me. I wasn't angry or hurt or upset, period. I would remain coolly civil because he had, reluctantly, offered me shelter from danger.

Ten minutes later, Gunnar carried Maisie in his arms and deposited her in the backseat.

I turned around in my seat to face her. "Hey kiddo, how are you feeling?"

She looked up at me with the saddest blue eyes and sniffled. "My tummy hurts, Peaches."

"Poor baby. We'll find the best doctor in Texas for you, just lean on your brother and take it easy, yeah?" She nodded but her brother glared at me. "No car seat so you have to stay back there with her."

I wasn't sure the law worked like that, but I knew Gunnar would protect Maisie with his life.

He gave a sharp nod and remained silent as I drove us, as fast as I could without drawing the eyes of the law, to the nearest hospital. Gunnar leaped from the car with the little girl in his arms, leaving me to follow or be left behind.

The nurse behind the desk gave Gunnar a bored look and handed him a clipboard, which seemed to scare the holy hell out of him. I smiled at the look on his face, taking pity and reliving him of the weight of Maisie while he filled out about fifty different forms.

"What's taking so damn long?" he complained when he was done.

"A four year old with a tummy ache isn't exactly a top priority, Gunnar." But the moans coming from Maisie broke my heart, and I handed her back to her brother.

"I'll be right back," I said.

"Where are you going?" he asked. It almost seemed like he gave a damn but I knew better.

"Don't worry, I have no plans to leave Maisie with no way home, Gunnar." But there was no way I could spend the next few hours listening to her moan in agony either, so I did what I did best and found a dark corner that would allow me to jump onto the hospital's Wi-Fi and perform a little magic.

The ER was packed, which surprised me in this small town. I couldn't in good conscious bump people with actual medical emergencies for her, no matter how adorable she was. But what I could do was add an appointment to the schedule of one Dr. Annabelle Keyes. It would cut into her lunch a little, but that little girl was worth it.

When I returned to the waiting room, Gunnar was still scowling at my seat as though I'd never left.

"You're here," he scowled.

I tried not to let his words offend me, but dammit, I was offended. "She's got an appointment with a family doctor in about three minutes, so we need to get up to the fourth floor. Now."

Dr. Keyes was younger than I expected with dark brown hair pulled into a tight bun with a pencil sticking straight through it. Her light brown eyes were friendly, and the dark green frames she wore overpowered her delicate features.

"What seems to be the problem?" She looked to me, probably assuming I was the mom or the nanny and I pointed to Gunnar.

"She's not feeling well," he grunted. "Says her stomach hurts and the school nurse said she has a slight fever."

Dr. Keyes checked Maisie out, keeping the little girl engaged in conversation about life in Texas, living with her brother, and all the guys at the ranch she had wrapped around her little finger.

"Sounds like you've got it pretty good, Maisie."

"Gunny's the best." She beamed up at him, her skin pale and her smile just short of a full beam.

After a short exam, the woman pushed her stool back and stood, extending a hand to Maisie. "The good news is that it's nothing serious, just a stomach bug. Nothing some Tylenol, clear liquids and rest won't cure."

She scribbled a few notes and handed the sheets to Gunnar before hurrying from the room.

"Thank you." Gunnar's words were sincere and the tired, terrified look in his eyes nearly made me melt. Nearly.

"I'd do anything for Maisie." Without another word, I held the door open and gestured for him to go first, since Maisie was once again, asleep in his arms.

"Seriously, thank you."

"Not necessary," I told him and averted my gaze. Gunnar had done me a favor and it took me until that moment to realize it. He was right, last night was just a physical release and nothing more. We shouldn't repeat it and that was all well and good, because when he wasn't being a total dickhead, Gunnar was kind of a nice guy.

Nice guys were trouble.

Too much trouble, and I had enough of that all on my own.

KB WINTERS

Chapter Twenty-Three

Gunnar

"So we're really doing this, becoming a motorcycle club?"

Wheeler was the most skeptical of the bunch because Special Ops guys were suspicious and cynical by nature. He kicked his feet up on the twin bed and grinned.

"Are we gettin' hazed or some shit?"

I shook my head and scraped a hand over my face, making a mental note to apologize to Cross for all the shit I'd given him over the years. Looks like it would be returned a hundred fold with these clowns. I'd asked Saint, Holden, Wheeler, Cruz and Slayer to meet in the bunkhouse to discuss what was next for Reckless Bastards, Opey, Texas Chapter.

"No hazing, just a probation period for all of you. Do what I say and prove you belong, which I know you all will, and we're good. Got it?"

They all had questions, and I tried my best to answer them because this was the start of everything. A new brotherhood. A new family. A new MC.

Cruz frowned. "I thought these clubs were only for white boys."

I snorted, but it was a common misconception.

"Some clubs operate that way, but the Reckless Bastards don't. The Mayhem chapter has some black members, some Hispanics and some white boys. All of them are the same Bastards no matter what color they are. We don't fuck around."

Cruz seemed satisfied with my answer, and Slayer clapped him on the back.

"What are you worried about, blue eyes? You're whiter than all of us." That sent everyone into a fit of laughter that would have been more in line in a high school locker room.

"Fuck you, Big Foot."

Slayer ran both hands through his long hair, shaking his head dramatically.

"Women love this hair, gives 'em something to hold on to when the dick just feels too good."

He rolled his hips and made a lewd gesture that made everyone laugh again and my shoulders relaxed. It wasn't official yet, but we were brothers.

"Better keep them away from big dick Holden over there or your dick will never feel *too good* again," Cruz joked and slid a teasing glare to the quiet cowboy.

Holden, for his part, flipped them off and went back to his sandwich. Holden already said he was searching for something more, something deeper and the MC would be just that thing.

"Any other questions?" Everything was in place. Cross had already sent the incorporation papers by messenger so everything would be official once they all passed prospect status.

Slayer raised his hand even though I'd told him not to do that shit because we weren't in school. He grinned when I glared at him. "What's going on with you and Peaches?" he asked.

I groaned, but all the others chimed in their desire to know the details too.

"Nothing. Cross asked me to keep her safe so that's what I'm doing."

Each of them received a deadly stare to let them know I didn't appreciate this line of questioning.

"Come on, Gunnar. We all know you're fucking her but what we want to know is are you gonna wife her up?"

"Fuck no. I ain't wifing nobody up, least of all a woman with trouble following her everywhere she goes."

That wasn't fair to Peaches, but when it came to who I let around my sister, fair didn't fucking come into play.

"That's harsh," Holden scolded. "We've all found trouble a time or two through no fault of our own, and Peaches is as solid as they come. Willing to help whenever she can. Plus she saved our asses on opening night."

That was all true, but beside the fucking point.

"Questions answered. If there's nothing else, we all have shit to do. Don't we?"

At my words everyone jumped to action, Saint and Slayer headed to the club to get it ready for the night's festivities, while Holden gathered the rest to help with ranch duties. We always had plenty of chores to do on a ranch this size, which meant our days were long as shit, taking even more time away from Maisie. It didn't matter that she was still curled up on the sofa, feeling sixty percent better. But for a boisterous little girl, it might as well have been six percent.

Another reason I wouldn't even entertain the idea of a woman or a relationship.

When all the guys dispersed, the ranch seemed too fucking quiet, and I made my way to the office inside the main house and sat down to do paperwork. Except I couldn't fucking focus and I knew why.

Peaches.

Holden was right about one thing. She was solid as fuck, helping me out with Maisie when I didn't deserve the help. She'd done more than she needed for The Barn Door, upgrading the surveillance system with an option to review the property and the club remotely, and even added security to the main house. I knew I didn't deserve any of it, not after the way I acted on opening night. I meant every fucking word, but in hindsight, I could have been less of a dick about it all.

Even the day she helped with Maisie, working her magic to make sure my little girl wouldn't have to wait all day to get home and into bed. I was an asshole. Something about the woman brought it out in me, and I needed to do better.

A car sounded in the distance and I didn't know why, but I was instantly on edge. And on my feet, heading toward the front door with the nine millimeter I kept locked in the office drawer. The car was nondescript, navy blue, four doors and boxy, just like the dark haired man who stepped from the car in blue jeans, heavy duty black work boots and a plain black t-shirt. Everything about the man screamed "government worker."

He spotted me and waved and I stepped onto the porch with my arms folded across my chest. "You lost?"

He flashed a smile and did his best to appear non-threatening which only made him seem like a bigger threat.

"Nah, heard you might have some cattle for sale?"

"You heard wrong." There was no way in hell he'd heard anything of the sort from anyone in Opey because the locals were dying for any information on who'd bought the Hardtail and what they planned to do with it. Martha never stopped talking about it.

"I won't ask you a second time. You looking for something?"

He held up his hands with an *aw, shucks* smile that was as phony as three dollar bill. "The name is Agent Farnsworth, and I have reason to believe you might know someone I'm looking for." He paused, I guess waiting for me to appear shocked or some shit, but I stayed silent.

"Name of uhm, Peaches? I wander if that's her real name. Do you know?"

"Don't know anyone by that name."

"You sure? Because I have reason to believe—"

"I don't give a fuck what you believe. I said I don't know anyone by that name, *Agent*. Is that all?"

He took a step forward. I pulled the gun from behind my back. "I said is that all?"

"I'm just leaving a card in case your memory returns."

"Not necessary. You have sixty seconds to get the fuck off my property." The best thing about Texas was that a man didn't just have a right to defend his family and his property, he was encouraged to do just that with very few questions asked and the weapon of his choice.

His dark brows rose, and even though his lips stayed fixed in a smile, I saw that hint of wariness creep into his gaze. "You'd shoot a federal agent?"

"Are you a federal agent? I didn't see a badge."

And that car didn't have government plates. In fact, it was more like a car that was trying not to be too flashy and draw attention to itself. When the asshole didn't produce a badge, I aimed the gun right between his eyes. "Thirty seconds."

He took a step back and then another. "You have no idea what this woman is involved in and if I were you—"

"You aren't me, so don't presume to tell me what the fuck to do, think or feel. Twenty seconds."

"She's committed some serious crimes buddy. This won't end well for you. Or your little girl."

I could have let him get to me. I wanted to jump off the porch and pound that motherfucker into oblivion. Instead I aimed at the rock beside his foot and shot. "I see you around here again the next shot goes between your eyes."

"I'm leaving."

"You have five goddamn seconds so I suggest you hurry the fuck up." The fucker finally got the message, ran for his car, and slammed down on the gas to get the fuck off my ranch before he even shut his driver side door. But that didn't stop the acid churning in my gut or the sense of doom that settled right beside it.

I'd come here to get Maisie away from this kind of trouble, this exact fucking danger, and it had followed me. No, not the danger, the woman.

Fucking Peaches.

Chapter Twenty-Four

Peaches

Three fucking days. That was how long I gave Gunnar to tell me about the guy who showed up on the ranch looking for me while sneaking in a threat to Maisie. Three goddamn days and he said nothing. Not one fucking word about the potential danger because at least one of the assholes had found me.

I thought long and hard about approaching him with what I'd heard, but another fight wouldn't help anything so I waited. And waited, hoping that Bob fucking Slauson would get off her fucking ass and call me to let me know what was going on. She hadn't and neither had Gunnar, goddammit.

Even Vivi didn't have any new information for me. I was getting worried and a worried me could be reckless, which was the last thing this place needed. We had vets suffering from PTSD, three women completely unable to take care of themselves, and a little girl who didn't deserve the trauma she would endure. All because of me.

I had to get away from here. For real this time. With me gone, the danger would bypass the ranch and follow me to wherever I headed next. The problem was getting off the ranch unnoticed, which was no longer possible thanks to all the security I'd added to the property. It wasn't impossible just...*difficult*.

I'd have to wait until Gunnar and the guys were busy at The Barn Door or those closed door meetings they'd been having more and more frequently. Only the Lord knew what they were up to in there, and I had enough problems of my own to worry about. But those meetings were my key and there was another one coming up soon.

That was when I'd make my escape.

"You can't." I turned at the sound of Martha's voice and found the older woman staring at me with a frown on her face. "Whatever it is you're thinking, you can't do it. Not to that girl and not to Gunnar."

It was on the tip of my tongue to tell the old woman to mind her own business, but Martha was a nice old lady so I shrugged. "You don't know what's going on Miss Martha."

"Maybe not, but I know a troubled soul when I see one and at this place. I'm surrounded by troubled souls. I know enough to know you're planning to run off like a thief in the night."

"My stay here was never permanent, Martha." I said the words as much for her sake as for mine. Being around Maisie made me feel light and free. Happy, even. "I have to leave. That was always the plan."

"No, you don't." Arms crossed with her chin lifted high in the air, Martha was doing a damn good impression of a bulldog. Short, stout and stubborn. "You don't," she insisted, her voice quieter this time.

I sighed and dropped down on the bed, happy that I was smart enough to shove my packed bags into the closet and away from nosy housekeepers and inquisitive little girls.

"I can't tell you anything other than I have to." I wouldn't waste my time arguing with her.

"Maisie will be devastated."

It was the only thing guaranteed to kick me right in the gut, the idea of hurting Maisie. "She'll be sad, and she'll probably even cry, but she'll start kindergarten, soon and then first grade, and then second and that's what matters to me."

Like everyone else in her life who'd abandoned her, Maisie would eventually forget about me, but I could live happily on the run knowing she was having a normal life. The kind I'd always dreamed about having.

"Oh dear, what kind of trouble are you in?"

"The kind that doesn't mind taking out any and every one in its path, Martha. Trust me, this is the best thing I could do for her. For you and your daughters too. For everyone."

"Everyone but you," she grumbled and took a seat on the edge of my bed right beside me. She bumped my shoulder with a sad sigh. "You can't fight this alone."

"Sure I can. I have to. It's how I fight every battle." And that was what this was now, a battle. Bob hadn't reached out ,which meant it was up to me to do something before the next person came looking for me.

"That's no way for a woman to live."

"It's the only way I know how, Miss Martha. You've been so kind since I've been here, thanks for that. But I need to do this, and I need you to keep this conversation to yourself."

I could see the hesitation and the instinct to argue in her light brown eyes. "Don't tell me you can't make that promise, Miss Martha. We both know if you tell Gunnar he'll go Neanderthal and try to fight this battle, which isn't his battle to fight."

The moment Gunnar stepped between me and the CAD, Maisie would be their target. I couldn't let that happen. I had to go.

"And what's so wrong with that? That's a man's job, to protect the people he loves."

Her soft wrinkled hands wrapped around mine, eyes deadly serious and equally fearful.

"He doesn't love me, Martha. My best friend is married to one of his closest friends and me staying here was a favor."

She still wasn't convinced so I went in for the kill. "He can't win this battle Martha, I almost certainly won't win it either, but I don't have a precious four year old counting on me."

I knew the moment the words registered, because tears began to well in her eyes. "You mean?"

"Yes. I probably won't make it out of this last bit of trouble I've found myself in, and if Gunnar tries to help, he won't either. That's why I have to leave. Soon."

Her shoulders fell in defeat, and I relaxed just a little. "You're wrong about one thing, that little girl is counting on you. I don't know if you've noticed, but she's crazy about you, thinks you hung the moon, Peaches."

I smiled. "She means the world to me, and that's exactly why I have to leave. Gunnar came here to give her normal, and that's exactly what she'll have." One way or another.

"I'll keep your secret for now, but not forever."

"I don't need forever, Martha. Thank you." Because she looked like she needed it, and maybe because I needed it, I leaned in and hugged her tight. "Everything will be fine."

"Everything but you?" One tear slipped from her eye and it gutted me. No one had ever cried for me before because no one had cared enough to, except Vivi, but she was too tough to cry.

I nodded and flashed a small smile at the kind older woman. The fact that Martha's tears were for me only strengthened my resolve to leave. The further away I was from the people on Hardtail Ranch, the safer they would be.

"There's only one person who'll miss me Martha, and she's got her own life now."

If I made it out of Texas alive, I'd call Vivi one last time before disappearing. Forever.

Chapter Twenty-Five

Gunnar

It was a rare quiet day on the ranch and things felt oddly calm, a feeling that took some getting used to. At first. But after a long, lively breakfast with Maisie followed by a couple hours helping Holden and the guys with the ranch chores, a relaxing rest of the day was just what I needed. The fact that I didn't even remember what it felt like to be relaxed didn't seem to matter one damn bit because the closer I got to the main house, now with a light yellow paint job requested by Maisie, the stranger it seemed until I realized why.

Peaches. The woman was normally everywhere, in very few clothes making it damn near impossible to ignore her. To avoid her. Both of which I'd been doing for a while now.

At first it was anger because that asshole showed up looking for her, and then it was simply self-preservation. But without Peaches in my face, bugging me, and making me laugh, making me want her, things were a little too damn dull.

My smile hit the moment I set my foot on the bottom step of the back porch. It only grew as I climbed the stairs and pushed into the kitchen, certain I'd find her having coffee and cake over a chat with Martha.

But she wasn't there. Neither was Martha for that matter. "Martha?"

No answer from her either, but the sounds coming from upstairs took me to Maisie's room. If there was one person who would always know where to find Peaches, it was her. "Hey Maze...where'd all this stuff come from?" Her room looked like Christmas in July. Presents everywhere. Clothes and shoes, a pink laptop, toys and even a guitar.

Her big blue eyes were as happy as I'd ever seen them as she held the little guitar in her hands, pigtails lopsided as they always were. "Peaches bought it for me. She said it was because I'm such a good girl."

"She's right about that. You are the best girl," I told her and tapped her nose with my finger. I knew Peaches loved Maisie, but something about this felt off. "Did you thank her for all this?"

She gave a big embellished nod. "I did. Want to learn to play guitar with me?"

My gaze went from the guitar in her hands to the little blonde girl on the paused screen behind me. "In a minute. Have you seen Peaches?"

Her little face twisted the way it did when she was deep in thought trying to remember some detail. "Uhm, yeah but not since she said she was going to help Martha hang the laundry out to dry."

Hmm. That explained why Martha didn't answer earlier. "Thanks Maisie. We'll play guitar later, okay?" My feet were already on the move but her question stopped me in my tracks.

"Promise?"

I turned to face her and arched a brow. "I promise. Stay here, Squirt. I'll be right back. Love you."

"Love you too, Gunny!"

I shook my head as I jogged down the stairs, knowing she would be calling me that damned nickname until the day I died. Those thoughts were pushed aside as I ran down the front steps headed towards the bunkhouse, but the sound of a familiar ringtone stopped me. "Cross, I can't talk right now brother. I'm trying—"

"This ain't a social call, Gunnar. Jag just got notice that Bob Slauson was found dead in her car on the side of the road. They're calling it a heart attack, but she had a bullet in her head."

"Shit!" His words sank in instantly and dread rose up in me, making my feet move like they were trapped in mud as I tried to get to the bunkhouse.

"I haven't even told her about the guy who visited last week looking for her." Now I felt bad because she'd had no warning that the people hunting her were so close, but I knew if I told her she would leave. And I didn't want that.

"What did you tell him?"

I stared at the phone to make sure this was my old Prez, Cross, I was talking to.

"You seriously have to ask me that? I didn't tell him a goddamn thing, not even confirming that I knew the name. You know me. At least I thought you did."

Cross sighed. He sounded exhausted, making me realize what a dick I'd been about all of this. "I do know you Gunnar, but I also know you're no fan of Peaches."

And what he didn't say was that I was perfectly fine with Vivi doing the Reckless Bastards' jail time for us because I was no fan of hers either. Even though she'd proven herself more than worthy.

"How's she doing?"

I shrugged even though he couldn't see me, and I wondered if I would always feel like a subordinate where Cross was concerned.

"Hell if I know. I think she's avoiding me because I haven't seen her in a few days, even at meal time."

Just then I thought of all the gifts she'd gotten Maisie, and I had a sinking feeling in my gut. They were years of birthday and Christmas presents. "Shit."

Cross groaned, expecting to hear the worst. "She's not answering Vivi's calls either, and this morning, she got rid of that number. Gunnar, I need you to get eyes on Peaches, man. Now."

I didn't know who hung up first, me or Cross, because blood pounded through my head as I ran to the bunkhouse, finding everyone there but the woman I was looking for.

"What's up, man?" Saint was the one to ask the question, shocking the shit out of me. If I'd been thinking straight at the time, I would have realized what progress he'd made but my mind was full of one woman.

"Peaches. Have any of you seen her today?" Holden sat around the table with Saint, Slayer and Ford, already getting a head start on playing cards and drinking beer.

"Nope." They all had a variation of no which only pissed me off.

"Fuck." I hesitated for a minute, wondering if this was a burden I needed to place on these men right now. But this was an emergency and even when his PTSD was at its worst, Max had been there when we needed him.

"Peaches is gone."

I told them about the guy showing up last week and as much as I knew of the work she did and what brought her to the ranch. "I should have told you sooner but I was hoping it wouldn't come to this."

Only Holden gave me a look that called bullshit, because he knew that her stay was meant to be much shorter so there would've been no need to tell them anything.

"So she's hot as shit and a badass?" Slayer snorted and shook his head. "No wonder you're so fucking scared of her."

I glared in his direction but the fucker was unfazed. "We need to find her." At my words, they were all on their feet, shoving them into shoes and boots, grabbing jackets and gear. Ready to help.

"Thank you," I said before we all hustled out of there.

"None necessary," Holden said as he clapped me on the back. "We're brothers, remember?"

"Fuck yeah," I told him, my expression serious as we shook hands and embraced the way men do. The way brothers did. I walked out and tried to call Peaches, knowing ahead of time that it wouldn't go through, yet still pissed when it didn't.

"The number you have reached is no longer in service."

She'd made it damn near impossible to find her, and she was damn good at disappearing according to Jag and Vivi.

"Shit! Shit! Shit!" My stomach lurched and it became hard to swallow as bad thoughts, terrible, deadly thoughts ran through my mind, all involving Peaches, pale and dead. Alone.

Holden stepped up and placed a hand on my shoulder, a sympathetic smile on his face. "It's better to realize it now than when it's too late, brother."

"What?" There was no need to bark at Holden because the man let shit roll of his back like melted butter.

He grinned. "That you're in love with her, dumbass. It's better to figure it out before it's too late. Believe me." There was a story there and if I wasn't so worried and so damn selfish, I would dig.

"I'm not touching that comment, not even with your foot long cock, Holden." He laughed and pushed me towards the ATVs in the barn because they would help us search the property quicker.

"As long as your heart knows it, you don't have to say a word, least of all to me."

That was the last thing Holden said before we took off to find Peaches.

The woman I might—or might not—have been in love with.

Chapter Twenty-Six

Peaches

I wish I could have said that it had been far too long since I'd slept in a car but that would have been a damn lie. That went double for the half-rusted piece of crap pickup truck I traded the Caddie in for. It was old as hell, too old to have any trackable technology, which suited my purposes just fine, but it was the second worst place I'd ever slept.

After I'd picked up the truck last night, I pulled into a truck stop for some food and planning session. I needed something that at least resembled some kind of getaway plan before those assholes caught up with me. I still couldn't believe Gunnar hadn't said anything to me about the man showing up at the ranch.

But first, I had to switch the license plates just in case they somehow figured out how to find Ray from Craigslist who'd always wanted an old Cadillac, and he gave them important information. Temporary out of state plates were the best in this situation because most cops didn't know enough about how other states worked to make a big deal out of it. Also, they were easy to change out quickly. I also got rid of my phone, shoving it into one of the airholes in a trailer that made sure livestock arrived at their destination still breathing.

Over a big fat juicy cheeseburger complete with a salad and chili fries, I read an anonymous email, encrypted up the ass, telling me that Bob Slauson was dead. There was no other information and I couldn't be sure it wasn't a trap so I fired up the old search engine and my heart fell to my gut at the words on the page. A heart attack, so they said, but Bob would never do something as amateurish as pull over on the side of the road in the middle of the night. Not for anyone. She'd done too much shady shit in her life to ever take that risk. Someone took her out. A hit. I was literally and figuratively fucked.

Bob was the only protection I had and now that she was gone, I was truly on my own. No wonder that guy hadn't been worried about showing up so brazenly at Gunnar's place. Fucking prick.

Once the sun came up, I drove into the closest city and found a cheap, by the hour motel to get cleaned up. Homeless street urchin wasn't the look I was going for when I needed to play nice with the good ol' boys to get my hands on some firepower.

God bless Texas, was my only thought as I drove along the interstate, clean, powdered, and perky again, and finally spotted a giant hangar that simply said GUN DEPOT.

"Thank you, Texas!" I grabbed one of my IDs and shoved a few stacks of cash into my bag before popping a few buttons on my red and white checked shirt and hiking my denim skirt up just enough to cause a distraction.

It worked. Ninety minutes later I had enough weapons and ammo to start a small army. It was just me, which meant this should take me as far as I could go with what I was up against. I loaded up the back of the truck, covered and secured it and got back on the road, driving a few hours in the opposite direction, hoping that zigzagging across this huge ass state would throw them off my scent.

It was already after lunchtime when I came to a stop at the urging of my growling stomach, but before I could even think about food, there was something I needed to do first. I opened one of the burner phones I'd bought and dialed the only number I knew. "It's me, Vivi."

There was a long silence and then a loud gasp. "What the fuck were you thinking, Peaches? Leaving the Hardtail Ranch! Leaving, really?"

I thought she might've been done but I gave her a second just to be safe.

"Gunnar is worried sick. He called us to see if you were headed here. Imagine my surprise because I haven't heard a fucking word from you in days. Almost a goddamn week, Peaches!"

"You done?"

"For now. Seriously, what the fuck?"

"I had to figure a few things out. That's why I didn't call. Besides, you said *you'd* call if you heard anything and you didn't. Not even about Bob."

"Not that you'd know, since you cut your goddamn phone off."

She was right, but so was I. "So you're saying if I check the messages, I'll hear your voice telling me Bob's dead?" She didn't say anything and I didn't even have the energy for a stupid smirk. "That's what I thought."

"Okay fine, I knew if I told you that, you'd fly out of there like your ass was on fire. And look at you fly, girl."

I snorted and rolled my eyes. "Since when are you such a drama queen? Anyway, I found out about Bob early this morning and I was already gone."

"Clearly," Vivi grumbled but I heard the telltale sniffling again and I was alarmed. "You're my sister and you weren't even gonna say goodbye?"

"That's what this call was supposed to be. I didn't think Gunnar would notice for a few more days." Barely thirty-six hours had passed since I snuck off the ranch, but I figured he wouldn't notice until tomorrow some time. "He's more perceptive than I thought."

"And he probably wouldn't have if Cross hadn't called to tell him about Bob." Vivi was pissed and although I understood why, I couldn't deal with it right now.

"I had a few errands to run first to make sure this was the path I wanted to go down."

"And now you're sure?" I heard her skepticism, but I wouldn't let her know it got to me.

I wasn't sure, not even a little bit, but this wasn't really about what I wanted. This was what had to be done. "Absolutely."

"Well I'm not, dammit. Go back to the ranch. Please."

"I can't." As much as I didn't want to spend what could possibly be the last few minutes I had with my best friend arguing, I had to tell her the truth. I told her about the fed who showed up on the ranch and threatened Maisie.

"And Gunnar didn't say one damn word to me." She wasn't convinced, but she would be. "He was watching, just enough to know Maisie was his weak spot, but still, he didn't say shit to me about it, Vivi."

"Don't you think that's for Gunnar to decide?"

"Hell no, I don't. We both had parents who didn't give a fuck about the kids they brought into this world, Vivi. Look how we ended up! Maisie has a chance at something better."

Vivi snorted, and I could just picture her doing her best to look snooty. "We didn't turn out so bad."

"Maybe not," I conceded since Vivi was living as close to normal as people like us were allowed. "But she has a chance at better than fifty-fifty. Maybe even better than your somewhat normal life and damn sure better than making a goodbye call to your best friend before your Dirty Thirty."

Vivi was no longer just sniffling, she was out right crying. Blubbering, even.

"Don't say that Peaches. I can't hear it, not now."

"Wow, chica, pregnancy has made you soft."

She snort-laughed on the other end of the line. "That's what carrying life inside of you does to a woman."

That thought made me smile, and I was glad I didn't stay in Mayhem and bring this shit to her door. "Then you do have something else to worry about right now. That baby. Not me."

"Don't hang up yet, Peaches."

This was hard. It was the first time we'd ever said goodbye to each other where it might actually mean goodbye. Listening to my best friend, the toughest chick I knew, cry her eyes out over me, tore my heart right out of my chest.

"Take care of yourself Peaches. Be safe and call me from wherever you land next."

It was what she always said before one of us left on a job we couldn't talk about or a vacation that was meant to erase another scar. This time it was bullshit. We both knew the next place I'd land was the morgue, but I smiled and nodded even though she couldn't see me. I wasn't sure how pregnancy hormones worked, but I figured it was better safe than sorry.

"Will do, Vivi. Take care of that baby. Love you." I ended the call before she could say something that would make me change my mind. I sat in my car and let the tears fall. And fall. I didn't know how long I stayed there, but I stayed until I was all cried out.

I washed my face with a bottle of water, changed into my favorite worn out jeans and got back on the road, headed somewhere.

Anywhere.

KB WINTERS

Chapter Twenty-Seven

Gunnar

"You didn't think I'd let you get away so easy, did you?"

I could have kissed Jag after he called with news of Peaches' whereabouts and more importantly, her phone number.

Peaches laugh was deep and husky but it lacked her usual amusement, hammering home once again just how much trouble she was in.

"But I did get away, Gunnar. The words you're searching for are 'thank you'."

What the fuck? I looked at the phone like it might sprout a head. "What am I thanking you for, exactly? Sending me all over the ranch in search of you or having the guys run all over Opey and beyond searching for you?"

She laughed again, this one was colder and darker. More distant. "For taking my troubles away from you and your family."

I could tell by her tone that she actually believed that shit, which pissed me off for a couple reasons. First, because it meant I'd misjudged her and she wasn't saying that shit to get sympathy and second, well, because she believed that shit.

"We've all been searching for you, Peaches. Maisie is—"

"No. Stop. Don't tell me." She was on the verge of tears, something she hadn't done since we'd met, and that was a good thing in a woman as far as I could tell.

"Fine," I conceded because like most men, I was shit at dealing with emotional, crying women. "Where are you?"

"Somewhere safe." Vague words meant to piss me off or protect me. Didn't matter, the outcome was the same.

"I've been going crazy trying to find you. I thought those assholes had gotten to you." My voice broke, showing even her just how worried I was about her. "Just tell me where you are."

"Careful Gunnar, you almost sound like you give a damn." I could hear the smile in her voice in her attempt to lighten the mood but I couldn't.

Not this time. "Of course, I give a damn."

She was silent for a long time, so long I thought maybe the call had dropped, but the timer still ticked. I waited her out, wondering if my words scared her, appealed to her or pissed her off.

"I'm fine Gunnar. I'm armed and making plans as we speak. But I am glad you called."

She sucked in a deep breath and I could just picture the rise and fall of her tits, probably barely contained in a lowcut tank top or a tight tee.

"Thank you for putting me up for so long. I know you didn't have to, and I know I didn't make it easy, but I'm glad you did so, thanks. You have a good thing going on at Hardtail, and I hope it all works out for you guys."

A dark frown crossed my face at her words, and I ignored the searing pain behind my eyes and deep in my chest. It felt like anxiety and panic and fear. I fucking hated fear. "Sounds like you're trying to say goodbye to me, Peach."

"I'm not trying, Gunnar. I'm saying it. Goodbye."

"No, dammit—" But it was too late, she'd already ended the call. I called her right back. "Damn stubborn ass woman!" The call went straight to voicemail. Three fucking times it went to voicemail. On the fourth try, the operator said the number was no longer valid.

"Fuck!" I shouted. I wanted to tear my office apart until I felt better, until some of the anger and fear simmering just under the surface was let loose. Uncaged. But cleaning it up later would only piss me off and this room was off-limits to Martha and her daughters.

"Everything all right, Gunnar?"

I looked up and was met with Holden's steady brown gaze. Arms folded and eyes filled with concern, the cowboy was good in a crisis.

"Fuck no, I'm not all right. I finally talked to Peaches and she's gone. Said goodbye and then shut off her fucking phone. Fuck!"

Succumbing to emotions, I slammed the phone against the wall, but even the crack and shattering that followed did nothing to make me feel better.

"Did you tell her?"

I knew what he was asking, but I wasn't ready to talk about that. Hell, I wasn't sure if I'd ever be ready for that conversation. Thankfully, Holden didn't want to talk about it either.

"You have visitors." His tone was solemn and that got my attention.

"Look at this sad bastard, Max. Looks like we got here just in time."

I blinked to refocus my eyes. I had to be hallucinating or sleep deprived because it looked like two of my oldest friends had just strolled into my office.

"Cross. Max. What the fuck are you guys doing here, not that I'm not glad to see you ugly bastards."

We shook hands and then I hugged both men.

"You sounded like you might need some help, and Max and I were in the area. Thought we'd stop by and see this ranch we've heard so much about."

Cross was so full of shit and we both knew it, but goddamn it was the sweetest fucking lie I'd ever heard.

"How are things?" Max asked in that quiet, all seeing way of his.

"Shitty. Just got off the phone with Peaches, and she didn't tell me where the fuck she is. Said I should be grateful she's gone, thanked me and turned off her goddamn phone." How could she be so reckless with her own life?

"That's rough," Max conceded. "But I get why she left."

Max held up his hands to stop the tirade forming on my lips.

"She loves Maisie, man. It's as clear as day and as a parent myself, I would live at the bottom of the ocean if it would keep my kids safe."

"All ten of 'em," Cross muttered before Max confirmed that Jana was pregnant. Again.

"If we can stop talking about my spectacular love life," Max joked, "Jag called about an hour ago with a lock on her location."

That was good enough for me. "Where is it?" He named a city near Lubbock, and I groaned. "That's at least four hours from here. She could be anywhere by the time we get there."

Holden nodded; his expression serious. "Yeah, Lubbock is the only place she'll be able to fuel up, sleep or eat. An old buddy of mine has a charter business with a helicopter, but he doesn't work for free."

"Perfect. Get him on the phone and tell him we'll pay extra if we're gone within the hour." Holden held whatever comment he was about to make and walked off to make the call.

Cross clapped me on the back with a wide smile and laughing blue eyes. "You're already sounding like a Prez, man. Congratulations."

"Thanks, brother. I learned from the best." That much was true. I'd learned a lot from Cross, a fact I hadn't realized until the band of misfit veterans showed up on my ranch.

"Damn straight you did."

His grin was wide, cocky. The old Cross, the one I knew before his wife and kid were killed. That smile dimmed quickly. "I'm sorry about Peaches."

"I just want her safe," I said automatically. The lie came so easily even I wasn't sure if it was really a lie or not.

"Sure ya do," he smirked. "Moon says women who've been broken too many times are the hardest to love."

Max snorted from his seat on the raggedy sofa in the corner of my office. "Replace women with men and she could be talking about you, Cross."

He flashed a wide grin. "That must be why she always says I'm so damn worth it."

His gaze softened and for the first time since she came into our lives, I was jealous of what Cross had with Moon. He gave me a look to make sure I understood his words and I nodded.

"What do you need, Gunnar?"

I looked into his serious blue gaze and told him honestly. "To find Peaches." I told them everything I could remember about the guy who showed up looking for her.

"He wasn't a pencil pusher or a soldier. This guy was a hired guy, skilled and smooth. Probably deadly too."

Holden's heavy footfalls sounded, his boots loud on the hard wood floors. "It'll take us fifteen minutes to get to my copter guy, and we can take off in 45."

My shoulders fell as it finally sank in that in a few hours, I would set eyes on Peaches. "Thanks, man. I need you to gather up the rest of the guys. And I need someone to take care of Maisie."

Holden nodded and disappeared from view once again, proving what a valuable brother he was to have around.

"We have time for a quick tour?" Cross looked hopeful, and since we had a few minutes to spare, I grabbed my keys with a smile.

"We'll start at The Barn Door." Knowing I would soon have Peaches in my sights allowed me to relax a little and show off for my friends.

Chapter Twenty-Eight

Peaches

After Gunnar's call, I spent too much time coming up with plans that sounded good on paper. Mostly they consisted of running, but instead of plotting a direct path over the border, I decided to drive west until I hit California. There I could easily get lost in the crowds of people visiting the border every day, and leaving Texas behind would ensure trouble was far, far away from Hardtail Ranch.

I decided to wake up early and drive west, but a flat tire from all the glass in the parking lot postponed those plans. After walking three miles to the nearest tire shop, buying an old used tire and paying one of the employees to drive back and change it for me, it was close to dinner time. I needed to decide what came next. Did I leave now or wait until tomorrow morning?

My thoughts drifted all over the place while I weighed my options, starting with Gunnar and the call last night. He'd actually sounded worried about me, maybe even scared for me, which was un-fucking-settling. Was it all some ploy to get me to come back to Opey, or was he being genuine? Thoughts of him being sincere invaded my mind and had me wondering things I had no business wondering about.

Like, would things have been different if we were different people? Or would he have hated a girl like me on principle alone?

Not that I could blame him because I'd gone and done exactly what he was most afraid of. I brought trouble to his front door. Literally. And that thought dominated every other thought I had about Gunnar. It didn't matter what my feelings were; leaving was the right thing to do. No matter what his twisted sense of nobility thought about it. He didn't need to get himself in the middle of my crap, period.

Leaving was the right thing. I told myself that all afternoon and into early evening. I said it again when I left to pick up too much food for one woman to consume and one more time for good measure as I dug in and put a big dent in all that food. But just as my food coma set in, so did a massive bout of paranoia. I jumped up, grabbed my already packed bags, stuck my leftovers in bags, and got in my truck. I got on the interstate and drove, certain that staying in that particular shitty motel would end badly for me. Sooner, rather than later.

When I got about fifty miles away, I slowed down, driving with a purpose but not like a maniac.

"Shit," I whined to a roadside I recognized. I'd ended up right where I'd been the day before, and I needed to stop for gas.

"Get it together, Peaches," said a stern voice in my head. I shook off the fear after several deep breaths, glancing over my shoulder to see if anyone was following me. I made sure my gear in the back was properly covered and grabbed a few twenty-dollar bills from my wallet. I got out of the truck and looked carefully over my shoulder as I slung my purse across my chest and locked the door behind me.

There was nothing to be afraid of I repeated with every step into the gas station. I prepaid for the gas and grabbed a six-pack of water. After a quick trip to the bathroom, I was ready to hit the road again, but the sight of the driver's side door, wide fucking open, threw me for a loop.

Fuck. Fuck. Fuck. I froze and swiveled my head from left to right, letting my peripheral vision kick in to see who was nearby. But dammit, there was no one. Not even another customer to blame it on and that freaked me the fuck out. I didn't see anyone, anywhere, but standing in the middle of an open space seemed like a bad idea. I darted to the truck, ducking behind the wheel. I looked around; certain someone attached a bomb under it—maybe even under my seat. Fuck. Was it safer inside the truck than out?

I ducked down to see if there was anything under me. Luckily, there wasn't. I sat up slowly, peering out the window. I saw no one outside, so I grabbed my 9 mil and steadied it in my hand while I got out and walked around the truck, checking for evidence of anything. The guns and ammo were still in the back, thank God. It was probably someone in search of something easy to steal and sell, not deadly assassins.

"If it was them, I'd already be dead," I said out loud and nearly took off without my gas.

Five minutes later, I had a full tank and I put the pedal to the floor until I had enough distance between me and whatever the fuck that was for me to calm down. It was hot as balls both outside and inside the car, and that combined with the anxiety of constantly looking over my shoulder took its toll on me.

I was tired and bitchy so I stopped at the third motel I found that would accept cash. It was fifty miles in the wrong direction, but at least it increased my chances of surviving the night. I hoped.

***

With all three door locks engaged, plus the bar guard, I felt confident enough to extend my hot shower by a few extra minutes. The whole bathroom filled with steam, and my skin turned red from the hot water, but I let it rush down my skin, cleansing the last few days off of me. I needed to wash off the other motel, the time on the road, the gas station bathroom and honestly, life in general.

It was a nice shower, a short reprieve from the constant worry of running for my life. The roadside motel on the other hand was cheap, shitty sleep, and seven minutes was about all the hot water available. I got out and wrapped the smallest towel I'd ever seen around my mid-section and stepped into the room just as the phone rang. Assuming it was Vivi, I rolled my eyes and answered.

"I'm not talking about any of this with you right now so if that's why you're calling, you can go relax or bang your man. Anything but worry about me."

I waited during a brief silence on the other end of the line before I heard a deep chuckle. A deep masculine chuckle. "Damn, you girls really do talk about everything."

The sound of Gunnar's laugh made my lips curl up. Damn him!

"The same goes for you, Gunny." If he was calling to try to change my mind or guilt me into going against my wishes, he could relax or do whatever it was he did when he wasn't scowling at me.

His laugh grew louder at the sound of his nickname. "Want to tell me where you are, Peaches?"

I shook my head even though he couldn't see me, though even if he could, in this towel he wouldn't be looking at my face.

"Nah. This way you'll have nothing to give them if they torture you for information. Because they will," I reminded him, just in case he forgot who was chasing me.

Gunnar didn't take the bait. "How about if I apologize for being an asshole. Would you tell me then?"

"Are you sorry for being an asshole?" I didn't think he was sorry, but a girl could hope.

"Yeah," he sighed and it was a deep sound, like he'd done some thinking about it before now. "I could blame it on my shitty mother and that would be true, but it ain't the whole truth."

"You just don't trust women." I assumed I hit the target. It all made sense from his instant dislike of Vivi, and me to his suspicion of nice chicks like Moon and Jana.

"Certain kinds of women," he clarified.

"Women like me? I see." I could hear the defeat and the disappointment in my own voice, and I hated it, a sign of weakness. If I couldn't be strong in the face of Gunnar, I was as good as dead against the hitmen. That thought had me standing up straight. What the hell difference did it make if he didn't trust me and considered me to be on par with his shitty, untrustworthy mother? None, that was what. "Apology accepted."

"That's it?" His tone was half angry and half incredulous. "That's all you have to say?"

"Ah, you want to fight? That's too fuckin' bad Gunny, because I'm too fucking tired to fight with you. Go find a new punching bag."

There was a loud bang on the front door that scared the shit out of me. Instantly, I reached for the gun resting under my discarded jeans. Still in my towel, I aimed the gun at the door and slowed my breathing. The pound sounded again and again, and I kept my breathing even and my hands steady.

"Open the goddamn door!"

"Gunnar?" I said his name into the phone, but his voice was coming from the other side of my door. What the fuck was up?

"Is that you, Gunnar?" His name left my lips in a shocked whisper. Slowly, with one hand, I undid each of the locks and took a step back. "Come in," I said but I kept the gun aimed at the door.

He stepped inside and froze, taking a careful step forward before kicking the door closed behind him. "What's, uh, goin' on Peaches?"

"Just making sure you're alone. What are you doing here?"

"What do you mean what am I doing here? You ran away from the ranch, and I spent a week hunting you down, I'm here for you."

I shook my head because that didn't make sense. "You're crazy. Once I left the ranch, you'd fulfilled your promise to Cross."

"Put the goddamn gun down!" His outburst didn't frighten me, mostly it just pissed me off.

"Why? Maybe I don't trust you as much as you don't trust me." It was petty as hell, I knew that, but I couldn't help myself. One of his brows arched in a sharp angle, and I lowered my arm. "You shouldn't have come."

"I was hoping to talk some sense into you, but I can see that would be pointless."

I gave a sharp nod. "It would. My mind is made up."

"Change it." He took a step forward, and so did I because I didn't let big sexy ass bikers intimidate me. Ever.

"No." I tilted my chin up, defiance rolling off me in waves.

"Stubborn woman," he said accusingly, which was pretty fucking accurate.

"Grumpy asshole," I shot back because, well, he was.

"Troublemaker," he said, this time his voice softer and more amused.

That sound sent a wave of heat crashing over me, settling deep between my thighs. "Cocky bastard," I told him, my voice huskier than I meant it to be.

"You know how cocky I can be," he said and closed the distance between us. I stumbled back on to the bed. In a split second, he was beside me, a slow smile on his face as his fingers slid through my damp curls. My only disappointment was that it wasn't the curls between my legs.

I moaned and let my head fall back when his lips touched the sensitive skin of my neck, instead of my mouth like I expected. His wet lips kissed and skidded across my skin. His tongue traced the swell of my tits until I gasped.

"Yes." The word rushed out of me against my will, but I didn't give a damn, not as long as he kept his mouth on my body.

Gunnar pulled back, his expression sincere and intense. "I'm so fucking glad you're all right." In an unexpected move, he wrapped his big ass arms around me and squeezed tight, surprising a squeak out of me. Then he pulled back again and cupped my face before his lips slammed down against mine, making me wet and breathless.

I closed my eyes and let the feel of his mouth heat my body and send my pulse soaring. The way his mouth felt against mine, trailing between my tits before he pulled one into his mouth with a groan.

"Fuck. Peaches!"

My lips curled into a smile as his mouth and that sweet, glorious tongue settled on my pussy. "You first, Gunnar."

He chuckled against me, making my thighs and my clit vibrate, and I arched into him, grabbing his hair that was just long enough to wrap around my fingers and pulling him close. The way his tongue moved up and down my clit, grazing over my opening in a teasing gesture that made my body shake with need. He did it over and over again until my toes curled and I crossed my legs behind his neck.

The sound of Gunnar growling while he feasted on my pussy was enough to send me over the edge in a violent orgasm that brought tears to my eyes. I convulsed against him, grinding and rolling my hips as the last of the orgasm worked its way to the surface. He laughed against me and peeked up with laughing eyes and a slick smile.

"That glad, huh? Good to know." I cupped the back of his neck and pulled him up until we were face to face, and I licked his bottom lip. His top lip. Then I leaned in and sucked his tongue until he groaned.

"Fuck woman, you drive me crazy!" He tore himself away from me but those blue eyes never left mine as he stripped off his clothes in record speed and climbed back on the bed. "Now it's my turn."

My legs wrapped around him instantly and his was there, slamming his thick cock into me like it was the only place he wanted to be. The connection this time was shocking in its intensity, sending waves of electricity all over my body. Even as he fucked me, hard and steady, until I was climbing the bed to get away from the pleasure, even while pulling him with me because it was too fucking good to leave behind.

"Gunnar," I moaned over and over again, like his was the only name I knew.

He smiled and sat up, holding my thighs wide while he fucked me and rubbed my clit with his thumb. It was too much and I could tell by the satisfied look on his face that he knew it too.

"I know, Peaches."

I didn't care. It felt too good to think about anything but how he made me feel. How he felt inside of me, moving and thrusting, making me feel better than I had in a long time. It was how it always was between us, hot and frantic and intense, but there was a rawness to it that I couldn't escape. It was unsettling and intriguing all at once.

"Oh, fuck!"

He smiled again and leaned forward, nibbling my nipple and sending me flying into the atmosphere, floating on a cloud of lust and filthy pleasure. And then I was coming apart, flying into pieces as Gunnar continued to fuck me, searching for his own release. He looked at me like he was trying to steal my soul and it was unsettling, but it only enhanced my orgasm. My body convulsed, shook, vibrated with a second wave of orgasm that triggered his.

"Oh. Fuck. Peaches. Fuck."

I closed my eyes with a smile, finally free of his intense gaze, and let the pleasure wash over me. It was too much.

Hell, it wasn't enough.

Chapter Twenty-Nine

Gunnar

"How did you find me?"

We'd finally come back to earth and settled into the bed wrapped tightly around each other. Our pulses had settled, our breathing had returned to normal, at least normal enough to talk. My shoulders sank in relief at her question because even though I had a passing thought about telling her how I felt about her, it scared the fuck out of me.

"Cross and Max showed up to help and then Holden came through with a helicopter that took us to Lubbock."

Her eyebrows rose. "Really? A helicopter?"

"Yes, really. We figured out we probably missed you by a couple hours." Driving up and down the interstate in a rented SUV and checking motels for her unforgettable appearance for hours hadn't accomplished shit except making us all sore and pissed off.

"Who's at the ranch? Who's with Maisie?" Her big, brown eyes filled with concern, pleading for an answer.

"Martha and the rest of the guys, including Max, but I left Wheeler in charge of safety."

"Good choice." She spoke in short sentences, her voice firm and resolute but distracted.

"You're still pissed," I said.

Leave it to Peaches to be mad that a man had to come save her.

"That you're here with me instead of on the ranch with Maisie? Damn right I am." She sat up and the blanket fell off, showing off pale brown tits, rock hard nipples. "I appreciate your concern Gunnar; it means a lot to me actually. But you shouldn't be here."

"Well I'm here now, and I plan to help, so fucking deal with it!"

Peaches had a knack for pushing buttons until a person exploded. I stormed off the bed as gracefully as possible while naked and slammed the bathroom door behind me. Splashing cold water on my face, I knew I had to calm down. Peaches wasn't a woman who responded well to aggression or demands. A stubborn woman who thought playing the martyr was the right thing to do, but that was only because she didn't know the truth. There was no such thing as martyrs, just pawns, sacrificing their lives for bullshit government stuff.

When I opened the bathroom door, I half expected to find the room empty, like she was never there at all.

"You can't handle this on your own, Peaches. No matter how tough or smart you are, this isn't a one man job." These guys probably had a big fat bankroll and wouldn't stop until the job was done.

But she hadn't take off, a good sign. She sighed and rolled her eyes, but not even she could hide the fear and the worry darkening them.

"Don't you think I know that, Gunnar? I don't know enough people in this whole damn world to help me defeat them. Even if I did, this isn't their fight. It's not even mine, but I'm in it. Alone."

"That's bullshit. You have me. And Vivi."

"Don't be stupid. She's pregnant, and I wouldn't bring this anywhere near her."

I sat down on the bed and reached out to her, ignoring the brief flinch before she relaxed.

"They're not gonna stop, Gunny. Until I'm dead or until my scent grows cold. I need to leave the country for that to happen."

Something like fear clenched in my chest and right in the center of my gut, churning a thick acid that made it difficult to swallow. "You can't leave."

"I have to. I'm the last one left, the last loose string."

Fuck. I hated hearing her talk like that, with such finality. "You're giving up?"

"I'm not giving up. I'm being smart." She leaned over and ran a hand down my chest as she pressed a kiss to my jaw. "Thanks for wanting to help, but you need to get back to Maisie. Now."

"Not without you. Why are you in such a hurry to get rid of me? Do you know something?"

A moment of fire flashed in her eyes, but she banked it quickly. Too quickly.

"See, why would you want to risk your life for someone you can't trust? Because that's what you'd be risking Gunnar, your life. Maisie's chance at normal."

Peaches pulled back, sadness only making her eyes more enchanting, and slid from the bed. She dressed carefully, pulling one item from her bag and slipping it on before pulling out another until she stood in leg sculpting jeans and a Ramones t-shirt.

"I do trust you."

She flashed a sad smile. "Don't start lying to me now, Gunnar. Honesty was one of your best qualities."

"You didn't have to buy Maisie all those things, you know."

She shrugged like it was no big deal, but to my sister it had meant the world.

"She deserved them."

I couldn't help but smile at that because I agreed, and I wanted her to have everything she wanted in this world. "She would have remembered you anyway."

I was glad she didn't try to deny it. "For a time," she shot back easily and it told me a lot about her that I hadn't realized. A lot that made me regret that I hadn't made more of an effort to get to know her while she was around.

"The toys will get her play dates, and she'll do the rest to make plenty of friends. To have a good life."

"Why do you care?"

She shrugged and turned away. "Soft spot for kids, I guess."

That was bullshit but Peaches was stubborn as hell and she wouldn't give up something so personal so easily.

"Christ, Peaches, don't be stupid. I can help you. Me and the guys can help you."

"You're letting the fact that you're a man fool you into thinking you have a choice here."

She turned to face me, her expression doing a good impression of a stone. "Go home, Gunnar."

Of course, my phone chose that moment to ring. It wasn't a call, but a message from Holden. "Shit. Looks like company is headed our way. Grab your shit."

Without another word, she turned, stepped into her sneakers, and picked up three bags.

"Let's go."

Peaches turned to the door and flashed me a look before looking at her hands. Her full hands.

"Right." I opened the door and she hurried out, making a straight line for a rusted out pickup. "What happened to your car?"

"Traded it," she said and tossed her bags in the back seat before sliding behind the wheel. "Later."

I was halfway to the car where Holden and Cross waited when I stopped and headed towards Peaches. "Stubborn bitch," I grumbled when I slid into the passenger seat.

"Buckle up. Or you can go ride with your friends," she growled. She'd put a baseball cap on so curls stuck out all around, but even with that mass of curls, I couldn't miss the sarcastic arch of her eyebrow. "Okay then," she sighed and slammed the gas, burning rubber as she cut a hard right out of the parking lot.

Thank fuck for quiet country roads.

Chapter Thirty

Peaches

After driving all night with Gunnar distracting me in the passenger seat beside me, I made a decision. It was time to fight back. I pulled over into the parking lot of a truck stop and hunched over my laptop to do what I did best. Letting my fingers do all the work.

Why in the hell should I wait until I was dead to sink CAD and every motherfucker involved? No one had stepped up to help me—to save me—dammit, and I was the one doing the business of keeping this country safe. My lips curled in amusement at that, because it was a lie we all told ourselves so we could get the job done. No matter how dirty the job was.

But that thought, the layer of grime and filth that working as a government contractor produced, reminded me of something else. The envelope I'd grabbed from 1st Constitution. A quick look at Gunnar's sleeping form confirmed he was still blissfully unaware, and I turned to my backpack and the hidden zipper where the envelope had been since I left the east coast. It was a plain manila envelope filled with other envelopes that had been sent to me over the past few months with explicit instructions not to open them unless I was asked to do so.

Well, fuck that.

None of them were still alive to give me that request. I unraveled the string closure and dumped the contents out over my keyboard. I watched as each envelope, a different color, weight and grade of paper, fell into my lap. The first envelope was green and contained a one-inch flash drive from Oz. He was a sound specialist so I wasn't all that surprised that the drive contained an audio file, but the photos from Cass were a real fucking shock. They were dark and grainy, obviously pulled from video footage but the images were of the man dressed in head to toe black leaving a Paris apartment I'd never forget.

"Shit." The word fell from my lips on a shattered sigh as I tore into the final, pink stone envelope that contained nothing more than a single piece of paper. A fucking email. From Bob Slauson to someone, G. Stranson. I didn't recognize the name, but the email made it clear that he'd been the unknown member of the Paris team. Armed with new information, I cracked my knuckles and stretched my neck muscles, and started digging.

Sometime later Gunnar woke up and scared the shit out of me. "What's going on in that pretty little head of yours?"

"Wouldn't you like to know?" I ignored the flutter in my belly at him calling me pretty and arched my brow instead.

Gunnar nodded, his expression serious enough to chase away all traces of humor or lightness.

"Fighting back," I told him because that much was true.

Hope shimmered in his deep blue eyes, making a small part of me wish that hope was for us. "Does that mean you're coming back to Hardtail with me? Because you could've said that before Cross and Holden took the helicopter back to Opey." He gave me an exasperated look and I rolled my eyes.

"No. It means that I don't have to wait until I'm dead to fuck them right back. To take everything away from them, whoever they are."

I had a few ideas, not about G. Stranson but about the string pullers, because I wouldn't give those fuckers the satisfaction of calling them puppeteers. I braced myself for anger or just a barrage of reasons why I should go back to the ranch and let him keep me safe. As if he could.

He stared at me for a long time but this time the look wasn't disdainful or filled with lust. It was unreadable which was pretty fucking unsettling.

"I'm driving the next shift."

"That's not necessary. I'm well rested enough to drive the whole day, but first I need food." A thirty minute nap had given me enough energy to keep going, some greasy food and coffee would get me the rest of the way.

"I'm not arguing with you about this, girl. You drove all day yesterday and who knows how long the days before."

I smacked his hand resting on my thigh. "I know how long, because I'm a grown ass woman capable of making my own damn decisions."

"Except it's not just about you, I'm here too."

I hated when people tried to use logic and reason against me. That was *my* move.

"Yeah well, no one asked you to come along."

"Some things don't require askin'." I tried my best to ignore the shiver his words produced or the way my belly tightened at the deep timbre of his voice, but something about his tone had me feeling hot and horny. Exactly the opposite of what I needed at that moment.

"You've been up all night driving and then all morning messing around on the computer. You need to sleep. Even Superwoman needs her rest."

He flashed a wink that made me groan. "Don't try to be cute with me. It doesn't suit you."

"I don't have to try. I'm naturally cute."

I rolled my eyes, wondering what in the hell had happened to produce this playful, flirtatious version of the grumpy bastard I knew.

"I'm driving," he said, and I knew that was final.

"If it means that much to you." I handed him the keys before yanking them back.

"You get them after I get food."

I shut my laptop and shoved it back inside its box, locking it before I jumped from the truck, ignoring once again the way my body responded to his deep masculine laugh.

"Gotta love a woman with an appetite."

I kept moving in the direction of the diner separated from the gas station by a partition that could barely be called a wall. Once inside, I took a booth near the back but with an excellent view of the truck. I needed a thick juicy burger so I didn't bother with a menu.

"What's the hurry?"

"My growling stomach, that's what." I gave Gunnar a look that dared him to say anything more and he held up his hands defensively. "Any other questions?"

"Yeah," he said, his tone challenging. Luckily the middle-aged waitress chose that moment to come take our orders.

"I need a minute." He told her.

I flashed a smile at him and then turned to the waitress. "I'll have a bacon cheeseburger, medium. Onion rings, a salad and the tallest ice water you've got please."

"All that?" Gunnar whistled and the waitress smacked her lips together in disappointment.

"Silly, man. I'll be back when you're ready."

"Wait, I'll have what she's having. Minus the salad and the water. I'll have a milkshake and a soda. Oh, and curly fries."

He flashed his most heart-stopping smile at the waitress who rolled her eyes and walked away, but I noticed her smile was a little brighter and her cheeks were even pinker than the blush already there.

"Guess I'm not the only hungry one," I joked, hoping he might forget our previous conversation.

"So, what's your plan?"

"I'm just trying to make things right. A lot of people got killed over what I thought was a mistake, but I'm starting to think maybe it wasn't." I wanted to share more with him, to tell him about everything I'd found but I couldn't. "That's all."

"Bullshit."

"That's the truth, Gunnar. You just can't see it because you can't believe I'd ever tell you the truth."

His shoulders sank. "You're never gonna let that go are you?"

I shrugged and took a long gulp of my ice water as soon as the waitress set it down. "The good news is that I probably will."

His expression hardened. "You're a pain in my ass but somehow I still want you around."

That warm fuzzy feeling worked its way into my blood and made me squirm.

"Gee, thanks. I think." I rolled my eyes and tried like hell to hold back another smile, but dammit the man brought it out of me.

"But I'd settle for you believing me since, you know, I've never given you a reason not to trust me."

"You're right."

"But?" There was a 'but' in there if I ever heard one and I rolled my hands to move him along.

"But you have trouble written all over you."

One big hand motioned toward me in a general move, and one side of his mouth kicked up into a sexy grin.

"Those curves and that wild hair, those plump red lips. Plus you're some secret government's government hacker. Like I said, trouble."

"And you don't like trouble?"

He made me sound sexy and badass, which felt amazing, but sounded bad. Terrible.

"I've been known to tangle with trouble a time or two, but with Maisie, I need to be better. To choose better."

"It's a good thing I didn't ask you to choose."

"No," he sighed. "You didn't. But it turns out you didn't have to."

He didn't look all that happy about it, which didn't feel all that great.

Thankfully the food arrived before he could say more because I just couldn't hear anymore. I dug in, devouring the burger and onion rings in an embarrassingly short amount of time.

"Damn that was good," I said when I finished.

Gunnar looked up with a smile that was...*damn*. It was the kind of smile that made a girl want to lick his lips.

"Sounded like it was."

"I'll wait for you in the truck." I stood and tried to pass him but Gunnar reached out and wrapped a hand around my waist.

"You're touching me."

The fucker swiped his thumb across the strip of exposed skin at my waistband with a slow, sexy smile.

"I know. I can feel how soft you are."

"This isn't gonna work, Gunnar."

"What isn't?"

"This whole seduction thing you're working at to get your way. It's not gonna work."

"It already is." He pulled back with another panty melting grin. "But I'm not trying to seduce you, just trying to get you to sit down until I finish my food."

"I can't help it if you eat like an old lady at teatime. But fine. I'll sit and help you finish those fries."

I flashed a grin at him that felt a little too real for a chick on the run.

Chapter Thirty-One

Gunnar

"Are you sure you don't want us to stick around a few days, make sure it's safe for you to sleep at night?" Cross and Max snickered, bumping shoulders like little girls.

"No, I'm good." Just to be careful, I looked at Peaches sitting legs crossed, on the glider on the front porch. She glared at me, still pissed that I'd detoured to Hardtail Ranch when she fell asleep.

"Don't blame me you fell into a food coma," I'd told her.

She flipped me off, sending Max and Cross into another fit of laughter. "If you're sure, man."

I wasn't, but Peaches would see that I was only doing what was best. For everyone. "Thanks for dropping everything to come down here. It was good to see you fuckers again."

"You never have to thank us for that, brother." Cross stepped in and took my hand, wrapping an arm around my back. "Glad to see you're settling down here. Maisie seems good."

"She is." Despite all my worries about screwing up my kid sister, she was thriving here in Texas. She had half a dozen guys to dote on her, a loving grandmother figure and her favorite woman in the world on the ranch. What more could she ask for? "Thank God for that."

"You're getting emotional in your old age," Max joked. "Feels good, doesn't it?"

I nodded, because hell yeah, it kind of did.

"I have something for you." Cross dug into his black leather bag and pulled out a big manila envelope and my heart rate accelerated.

"It's official. Reckless Bastards, Opey Texas Chapter."

"Fuck man, are you serious?"

He nodded and my inner kid leapt out, wrapping him in a big damn hug. "Thank you."

"You'll always be a brother, Gunnar."

We said our goodbyes and Wheeler drove them to the airport so I could spend time with Maisie after being away for so many days.

I turned, expecting to find Peaches still glaring at me, but I should have known by the way my shoulders relaxed that she'd gone inside. Once again, Peaches shocked the hell out of me. She hadn't run upstairs to the guest room, instead she was sitting at the table with Maisie. Smiling and looking like a wet dream in a floral dress, her damp curls spilling in all directions and no makeup on her face. The cherry on top of that sexy ass sundae was that she didn't have a bra on under her dress. Her tits jiggled freely beneath the thin fabric, driving me crazy.

"Did you ladies leave any food for me?"

Peaches looked up with a glare just for me but Maisie wore a bright, beaming smile and jumped from her chair.

"No more food, Gunny. We ate all the slider burgers and they were yummy!"

I picked her up and tickled her belly, loving the sound of her joyful laughter. "Then I better get one from your tummy!"

"No, Gunny! You have some."

"Martha left yours in the warming oven," Peaches said as she stood, ruffling Maisie's hair. "Check ya later, kid."

"Will you be here in the morning, Peaches?"

She froze and turned at the question, eyes soft and kind of sad. "Yeah kiddo, I will."

"Don't leave on my account." I didn't want her to leave, but I knew I was still in the shit house with her.

"You need some alone time with Maisie." She didn't give me a chance to say anything else before disappearing upstairs. I knew she was pissed, and I expected the cold shoulder for a while so I'd put up with it.

I dropped Maisie in her seat, grabbed my food and joined her at the table. It was damn good to be home, in my own bed and surrounded by my people. My things. "So kiddo, tell me about your day."

That was just the opening she needed to take a deep breath before spilling every detail of her day, starting with a sausage patty with a biscuit and grape jelly. "It was the best sandwich I ever had!"

I listened and chimed in with a response in all the right places while I enjoyed my sliders, mashed potatoes and corn on the cob. There was a long moment of silence that had me thinking maybe I'd missed some part of the conversation. "What?"

"I said why don't you marry Peaches? She'd be a good mommy for me 'cause she already is."

Thank fuck Holden chose that moment to interrupt us because how in the hell was I supposed to respond to that? "What's up, Holden?"

He tweaked Maisie's nose, making her giggle, before turning his attention to me. "Suspicious activity on the perimeter."

I was on my feet before the rest of the sentence was out of his mouth, heading to the gun closet and then right out the door.

"Stay in the house with the girls, Holden." I turned back to look him in the eye. "Keep Peaches inside this house. Whatever it takes."

He nodded, and I took off, confident they would be safe until we figured out who tripped the sensors. My heart thundered as I made my way to the barn where the ATVs were kept, with Cruz at my side. I wondered what in the fuck I would find out there.

"Anyone see anything?" I asked on the run.

"Nope. Ford and Slayer are already on the way and they have radios."

It took a few minutes for us to get to an area on the northeast side of the property, right along the fence. "What did you find?"

"Looks like a fucking kid," Slayer said, disgust in his tone as he pointed a flashlight at the debris. "Four bags of potato chips, candy, dead flashlight batteries and a half empty can of soda. Not a pro," he said, and I had to agree.

"Could be a diversion," Cruz offered. "Fuckers are dangerous because they work more often than they should."

I didn't disagree completely. "Slayer is right. At least one of the people after Peaches wants something from her, otherwise she'd already be dead. So would we," I told them because I was trying to be as honest as I could about this trouble. Peaches had drilled it into my head enough, whether I wanted her to or not.

"Damn. When Peaches does trouble, she does it big, don't she?" Cruz grinned and clapped me on the back. "I'll take the north fence before I head back."

"Thanks." We all took an edge of the property to check on our way back to the main house and bunkhouse, and for now it had to be enough. Tonight was our first theme night at The Barn Door and I had two hours to check everything over before the doors opened.

I checked on Maisie when I got back to the house, but she was already tucked in bed so I dropped a kiss on her head and ran to a steaming hot shower to loosen the aches in my muscles. Sleeping in a fucking car for two days was bullshit, and a dumb idea for a man over the age of twenty-five. My aches had aches and I still had hours to go before I could stop running, stop moving.

And I hadn't had one goddamn minute to talk with Peaches since we got back to Hardtail. She ignored me, after yelling at me that if I was gonna bring her back, she would've liked to ride in the helicopter with Holden and Cross. It was a fair point, but we both knew if I'd given her a choice, she would have run off without me.

Dressed in fresh jeans and a shirt, I was ready to head to the club to make sure everything was in order for the night. The club did a steady business, even though we were closed on Tuesdays and Wednesdays, and I wanted to keep the momentum going. Too lost to my own thoughts, I ran right into soft, feminine curves at the bottom of the stairs.

"Peaches. Just who I was looking for."

"Where else would I be, Gunnar?"

"You're still pissed. That's okay, you're hot as fuck when you're pissed off."

She wanted to argue and maybe I said it to get a rise out of her, but it was true. Before she could give me another piece of her mind, I pulled her close and slammed my mouth down on hers, kissing her deep and slow until her nails dug into my shoulders and her tongue danced with mine. Only Peaches could turn a kiss into an erotic experience and eventually I had to pull back or fuck her.

"Tonight when I get back, we should talk." There was so much I wanted to say to her and now I was sure of what I wanted to say. It felt right. Free. A smile touched my lips as a weight lifted from my shoulders.

Peaches smiled but it didn't reach her eyes, and the tone was all off when she said, "Sure." It was non-committal and if I had time, I might have asked a few more questions.

"See you later," I told her and ran back out to the ATV.

Chapter Thirty-Two

Peaches

I couldn't sleep. It was quiet as hell except for the low humming beat drifting in the air from The Barn Door, but still I couldn't sleep. It didn't have a damn thing to do with the fact that I'd spent the past two nights with Gunnar, one in his arms and the other with him right beside me in the car. No, it had nothing to do with that. It couldn't be because I was still pissed at him for being high-handed and stubborn, for thinking he knew what was best for me and for putting everyone on the ranch in danger.

Because of me.

It was stupid as hell. Sweet and kind of chivalrous, but those were just synonyms for stupid, weren't they?

He wasn't totally stupid though, hiding the keys and the car so I had no way of escaping except on foot. And even that wasn't possible because there was always a pair of eyes on me. Even now. Holden was downstairs on the front porch with a shotgun in his hand, looking every inch the menacing cowboy protecting his property. He should be at the club, not playing bodyguard to me.

I told him as much earlier after Gunnar took off, but he just flashed that aw shucks cowboy smile, tipped his hat and stood sentry on the porch. Even now, from my spot near the window, I could see him there in the darkness, nothing but the cherry of his cigarette visible as the moon passed behind the clouds.

Other than a few clouds in the sky, the night was beautiful. Almost magical in the still beauty of it, a thick layer of mist rolling across the land. The moon lit up the night once again, and I caught a flash of something, or rather someone, darting from the bank of trees near the driveway to the trees closer to the bunkhouse.

I banged on the window frantically, trying to get Holden's attention. He looked up and I pointed towards the trees.

"Someone's there!" I kept pointing with one hand and lifted the window with the other. "I saw movement, looked human."

Holden's look was suspicious at first, and I knew Gunnar had told him to make sure I didn't leave the house. Finally he stood and started towards the bank of trees and I stepped back, feeling a sudden urge to check on Maisie since Martha had the evening off. It was probably the kid the guys assumed was camping out on the property, but I needed to see Maisie.

To be sure.

Something felt off. I couldn't describe it, and I couldn't shake the damn feeling, so I listened to it. Slipping into my sneakers and grabbing my butterfly knife, I tiptoed down the hall to the little girl's frilly cowgirl-themed room. A shocked gasp came out on a rush when I pushed her door open. Maisie looked up with a terrified smile, sitting frozen on the lap of a smiling blond man.

A mildly familiar smiling blond man. "Who the hell are you and what are you doing here?"

He looked up, not at all shocked by my appearance, which told me the kid out there was nothing but a distraction. "I think you know the answer to that question."

He was low key and smug with that gun in one hand, aimed at Maisie. "You all right kiddo?"

"Peaches!" She moved towards me but the asshole gripped her shoulder tight.

"Ow!" she yelped.

"Watch it, asshole!" I wanted to gut that motherfucker for even touching her, but I had to take my time. Get her out of harm's way first.

"I'm just making sure she's comfortable," he insisted with a slick smile that was trying a little too hard to be innocent. "You are a hard woman to track down."

"Yet here you are."

He smacked his lips in an admonishing sound that was meant to make me feel chastised. All I felt was annoyed. And terrified for Maisie who had tears pooling in her big blue eyes. "You're too damn smart and that's your problem, but your weakness is that pregnant friend of yours in Mayhem. Well, that, and that NSA agent with a drinking problem he hides with a gambling problem."

So he'd caught me by listening to one of my calls to Vivi. And I always used a burner. She'd be so pissed to know that. Fuck, we needed to step up our security game.

"You're here so you must want something. What?" If he didn't want something from me, he could've put a bullet in me while I slept, gotten in and out without being seen. This was messy.

Desperate.

Desperate people made plenty of fucking mistakes so I just had to keep calm and let this play out.

He laughed. "You know what I want. The file." He squeezed Maisie closer, his smile never wavering. "Don't bother denying it."

"What file? The one of you murdering a U.S. citizen, because I haven't seen that file. But I've heard plenty about it."

"Don't fuck with me, bitch! I will rip this little girl to shreds right in front of you." He held the cold metal to her head, making Maisie cry out as tears streamed down her face.

"Okay fine, I know what file you're talking about, but I don't have it. After you showed up at the ranch, I sent it to the New York Times."

"Bullshit. I haven't seen anything about it on the news."

In for a penny, as the saying goes. "Yeah, they blew me off. But now that Bob's dead, I'm guessing they're fact-checking as we speak and getting plenty of no comment type of comments."

He didn't believe me, and I knew I needed to sell it for just a little longer. "It doesn't matter. They have the info and it will come out, before or after you do what you've come to do."

"So fucking proud of yourself," he sneered and stood, nearly dropping Maisie, who cried out again. "Find the file and I won't kill her in front of you."

"If anything happens to her, you'll wish you were dead. Gerald Randolph Stranson. Divorced father of four. It'd be a shame if you weren't able to see those kids ever again."

I might have a weakness, but he had four of them.

"I hold all the fucking cards, little girl." Just to make sure I got the picture, he pressed two fingers to Maisie's shoulder until she cried out.

I couldn't take it, watching tears run down her frightened little face, but I had to get her away from him. Safely.

"You might have the cards, but your name is the one piece of evidence no one has yet, and if you piss me off or kill me before I've adjusted the auto-send email to fifty four different media outlets, the world will know."

"You'll be dead."

"I'm dead anyway," I told him, ignoring Maisie's shocked gasp because I had to. "But I'll die happy knowing they got you too."

That much was true, and I hoped that sleazy bastard could see it in my eyes, that I wasn't fucking around.

"Give me the fucking file!" His outburst cost him, jostling and scaring Maisie, which made her pee herself. He dropped her and she headed right towards me, arms extended.

"Peaches!"

I saw his intent the minute Stranson raised the gun, and I took a step to the side, pushing her out of the room.

"Run, Maisie! Don't stop until you find one of the guys!"

"You bitch!" He smacked me right across the fucking face as I turned back to him, sending me staggering back against the wall.

I smiled and pushed off the wall as I slid the knife from my back pocket.

"I've been called worse," I assured him just in case he thought I still had any feelings left to hurt.

"Who's the bitch now?" I asked as I shoved the blade deep in his gut and took off running.

"Run now, and I won't stop until the girl is working in whore houses all over Europe. Asia. The Middle East. All before her tenth birthday."

His words stopped me cold and his laugh said he knew it.

"She's a weakness."

"You want the file? Fine, let's go get the fucking file, but if you put your hands on me again, I'll cut your dick off and shove down your eye sockets. Got it?"

He nodded and raised the gun so it was aimed right at my chest. "Try anything funny and you'll be dead before you finish the thought."

Once we were away from the main house, I could press my luck knowing that Maisie would be well protected. "As long as we understand each other."

I took a deep breath and one step forward, preparing for the longest fucking walk of my life.

Chapter Thirty-Three

Gunnar

"Where is she? Where the hell is she?"

Holden called thirty minutes ago with a call that no parent ever wanted to fucking hear, telling me Peaches was missing as Maisie bawled her eyes out in the background.

"Well?"

Slayer had gotten to the main house first and pointed toward the kitchen.

"Poor thing, not even hot cocoa could stop the tears."

I understood his baffled tone because hot chocolate was my sister's favorite thing in the world, and a guaranteed way to cheer her up or distract her easily.

I made my way toward the sound of her tears, dropping to my knees the moment I set eyes on her, curled up against Holden's massive chest.

"Maze, honey, how are you?"

"Gunny!"

She slipped from Holden's lap with all the energy of a coma patient, dragging her feet towards me before she flung herself in my arms.

"Gunny, the bad man had a gun and said he'd kill me if I didn't sit in his lap so I did. And then h-h-h-he wanted to take me but Peaches wouldn't let him."

She sniffled, her sobs growing stronger as she relived the trauma. "He scared me so bad I peed my pants and I r-r-r-ran to Peaches b-b-b-but she pushed me and told me to run away. W-w-w-why did she push me away, Gunny?"

Whoever said raising kids was easy had no fucking clue what they were talking about because her tone was enough to rip me in half, to tear my heart right out of my fucking chest. But to hear her cry like that, that nearly brought me to tears.

"She was trying to keep you safe, Maze. You know she loves you."

She nodded and wiped her eyes with a watery pout. "But she yelled, too."

"Because it was serious and she wanted to make sure you ran. And you did, didn't you?"

She nodded. "Right to Holden, but we was too late. Peaches is gone."

Gone. That motherfucker had gotten her and she'd put herself between him and Maisie. "You did great, Maisie."

"She's a damn fine cowgirl already." Holden's words pleased her and she beamed a smile up at him.

She gasped and turned back to me. "Peaches called him Gerald, and he got real mad, then he got madder when she said she sent the files to New York time. What's that?"

Now it all made sense. Why she was pissed but didn't fight me hard on staying at the ranch. She was planning to blow the whistle and disappear anyway.

"It's a newspaper, sweetheart." My gaze turned to Holden whose eyes were full of apology and fear and disappointment.

"Where were you?"

He sighed. "Found the kid camping out on the property and I mean kid. He's no more than fourteen."

"Fuck" It was more than I could deal with now, but this was the job of the club President. "Where is he?"

"Your office. With Mitch."

"Thanks. Anything else?" Holden shook his head and took a seat, shoulders sagging low. "Peaches said she had his file, somewhere else."

"The truck?" Holden said just as the thought crossed my mind. "What about the supply shed on the western pasture? Does she even know about it?"

I stood to take Maisie upstairs to my bedroom. "I have to try to find Peaches, kiddo. Slayer will stay here with you until I get back. Okay?"

She nodded, blue eyes still full of tears even though her sniffles had slowed. "Can I have hot cocoa now?"

"Sure but you listen to Slayer. If he tells you to do something, you do it. Okay?"

"I will Gunny. Love you."

"Love you too, Maisie. See you soon."

After I settled her in her room, I took off with Holden and Cruz at my side since Wheeler and Saint were still at the club. We made it to the small shed in record time, stopping a quarter mile away just in case the bastard wasn't alone.

"Don't worry, we'll find her," Holden said to reassure me.

"You don't know that, Holden."

He couldn't possibly know that. "Chances are this doesn't end well tonight." And I knew that because I had the feeling I had in my gut every time I'd lost someone. The men in my unit, my fallen Reckless Bastards brothers, and even my mother.

"If you believe that, what the fuck are we doing here?"

"I have to try, Holden. She put herself between death and Maisie. I owe her."

"I'm sure your gratitude will overwhelm her heart," Cruz snorted. Crouched low, he moved ahead of us quickly, checking the area for traps. And snipers.

I was glad the guys were so sure, but I couldn't be. Every fucking time I closed my eyes, there Peaches was, lying on the ground, pale with lifeless eyes, asking why I came too late.

"They're inside," Cruz whispered and motioned us forward to the door. "Listen."

A man yelled angrily. "You said it was here, goddammit!"

"No, I said it should be here. Clearly some kindhearted soul decided to clean and detail my piece of shit truck. Who knew?"

My lips curled up because that woman was pure trouble, talking back even when she was outgunned.

"Get me that fucking file."

"Get it yourself."

What the hell was she doing, goading the man into killing her?

"You think your boyfriend's gonna swoop in and save you? That's rich," he laughed.

"I don't need anyone to save me, Gerald. I'm bored. If you plan to kill me you better do it quick before the hunter becomes the hunted. Because you will. You know the rules."

"Just get me the fucking files, and I won't have to."

She barked out a laugh. "Sure hang on, let me grab the flash drive from my ass so I can save you."

"It'll be worth killing you just so I don't have to hear your fucking voice again."

Peaches continued to laugh and that was when Cruz gave the signal to get closer to our breach points.

A shot rang out before I kicked the door in and my heart got stuck in my throat.

"Not so easy to shoot someone who's awake, is it?"

She continued to taunt him. I could hear but I couldn't see shit in the dark shed lined with shelves.

I heard the smack. The punch. The struggle. As I made my way inside, I realized it wasn't a gunshot but tear gas. He knew we were here.

"It wasn't supposed to go down this way. Bob fucking Slauson," he yelled and another smack sounded.

"Not. My. Fucking. Problem." Each word was labored like she couldn't catch her breath even as she fought back.

I finally could see the outline of them in the back of the second room, boxes strewn everywhere and about five feet between them.

"Peaches!"

She looked at me the moment the shot rang out and sent her spinning before she fell to the floor in a dead heap.

"Oh. Shit." The sight tore a hole in my gut.

Seconds later two more shots rang out and the man fell.

"Get your girl," Cruz yelled and ran toward the fallen man, kicking his gun across the room.

"He's gone," Cruz shouted when he bent over to check on him.

"Good." My feet finally joined the party, carrying me towards Peaches' limp body on the ground. "Shit, you had to go and get yourself shot, didn't you?"

Her breathing was shallow but a welcome sound anyway. "My foster mom always said my mouth would be the death of me. Guess she was right."

Fuck no she wasn't. I couldn't hear that, not now. I shook my head. "Only you could joke like that right now. Don't even fucking think about dying, or I swear to God I'll bring you back and kill you myself."

"Seems. Inefficient," she tried to joke but her skin was pale and her breathing shallow.

"I love you, Peaches. I know this is the worst possible time to tell you, but it's true, and since you couldn't wait for our talk later, I'm telling you now."

I held my breath and waited for her to say something. To smile or frown, to hit me. Something. Anything.

"I must be dying if you're lying to me again."

"I'm not and you're not dying. I won't let you. Because I love you."

She rolled her eyes, but I didn't miss the joyful smile on her face.

"This hurts like a motherfucker Gunnar, I won't lie. I'm not dying."

"I know that, dummy. I figured I'd press my luck because you might be fuzzy enough to say it back to me."

I smiled, my heart full despite the way her blood oozed all over the floor, my hands and my jeans.

She smiled up at me, wincing from the pain despite the smile on her face.

"I must be feeling fuzzy then, because I love you too, Gunny."

Her right arm lifted up to cup my cheek gently. "Fuck, this really hurts," she said again and then passed out.

Chapter Thirty-Four

Peaches

I didn't know where the hell I was, never mind how I'd got there. All I knew was that pain radiated throughout my entire body, but mostly the back of my head. And my left shoulder? Fuck, it hurt like hell.

"Oh, fuck me!" Trying to sit up caused more pain and I couldn't even think about opening my eyes.

"Peaches you're okay. You're safe."

A feminine voice whispered soothing words at my side, grabbing my hand in soft petite hands. "Don't try to sit up."

The voice was familiar but I couldn't put a name to it, not while my mind raced trying to figure out how in the hell I'd gotten hurt. My eyes were shut tight as her voice continued to spout soothing nonsense words until I stopped struggling to sit up.

"I need you to relax, Peaches. You're safe now. Open your eyes. I've dimmed the lights so you should be able to open them now."

I tried to open them but a flash of memory came to me and they snapped shut. There was a guy with thick blond hair holding a gun on Maisie. Then on me. I sat up and let out a feral scream of pain as a thousand knives stabbed my shoulder.

"Why am I in so much pain?" I cried out.

"Open your eyes, Peaches. Now." The feminine voice was firm and commanding and slowly my eyes opened, one at a time. She smiled. "There you go. Welcome back."

The first time I saw her I thought she was mousy but there was an intellectual beauty about those kind honey brown eyes and her thick shoulder-length chocolate hair.

"Dr. Keyes. What are you doing here? How did I get here?"

Some shit must have gone down for my memory to have abandoned me. I wondered where Gunnar and the guys were, but I didn't know if I was ready for that answer. Yet.

"You're in one of the guest rooms on the ranch."

I was on the ranch. "The ranch? Where's Maisie, is she all right?"

I remembered that blond asshole with his gun trained on Maisie, like she was just a game piece. "Have you seen her?"

I know I sounded desperate, but I had to make sure she was all right, at least as much as possible after what happened last night. Was it even last night?

"I have, and she's fine. She was pretty overwhelmed and shaken up but she's sleeping now."

She was safe. That was good. Whatever else had happened, I was grateful to hear that. "Good. Thanks. How soon do you think until I can get out of here?"

"You've been resting for the past day and a half, but your body needs time to heal. That bullet tore through your shoulder pretty badly, tearing a few ligaments but thankfully, it went straight through."

I listened to her words with half an ear, wondering where in the hell Gunnar was, since he wasn't here by my side, making sure I made it through the night. If Maisie was sleeping, then he had to be around here somewhere.

"Why do I even give a damn?"

"Excuse me?" the doctor said.

"Nothing. What kind of drugs did you give me?"

"Painkillers and a sedative. Do you have any problems with addiction?"

"No, but I need my head clear. I've got to get out of here."

I needed to be able to think. I didn't know where the blond guy was or who might come after he was dealt with, which meant I needed to run while I could.

"No. You need to take a few days and let your body heal. This seems like a pretty great place to recuperate."

Of course it did to her. She wasn't abandoned by a guy who pretended to love her only when he thought she was dying.

"I just...never mind. So how long, in actual time, Doc?"

"Six weeks. That's how long your arm will be immobile. After that will be a few months of physical therapy, but I can't force you to do anything. However, I am recommending that you take a few weeks to do nothing but relax. No traveling, no working, no cooking, and no sex."

I snorted. "Not a problem, Dr. Keyes."

"Call me Annabelle."

I smiled. "That's it. Belle, you look like Belle from Beauty & the Beast. Tell me Belle, how did you end up here?"

She pursed her lips and took a step back. "That's something you should talk to Gunnar about."

I barely knew her but even I could tell she was being squirrely.

"I'm asking you. Tell me."

"A bunch of suits swooped in and forced everyone to sign NDAs and a bunch of other paperwork while quietly muttering words like treason and life sentence. They took that little kid and left something for you as well."

Annabelle handed me a thick envelope and I took it with a shaky hand.

"That doesn't tell me how you got here, Annabelle."

She smiled. "Gunnar and his friend Wheeler came to my house and begged me to come help you."

"You shouldn't have done that, Doc." Inside the envelope was an apology for the CAD mission and Gerald Stranson, a non-disclosure agreement with my signature already in place, probably from the signature in my file. There was also a check, a really big fucking check. It didn't make everything okay, but it sure as shit made me smile. Nothing would be okay after this, but the money would make everything easier.

"I guess that's it then."

"You sound disappointed."

"Not disappointed. Shocked a little."

It didn't feel like it was over, which was kind of fucked up. It was too easy to adapt to the bullshit, to get used to it.

"Did you have any other patients here at the ranch?"

"Some scrapes and bruises from the guys but that's it."

Big brown eyes cut to the door and my gaze followed hers. I had to hold in a groan at the sight of Gunnar, disheveled and frowning, like he usually was.

"I'll be right outside if you need anything."

Annabelle, the traitor, left like someone had just set her ass on fire.

"What are you doing here?"

"What do you think? I came to make sure you're all right." He scraped a hand over his head and blew out a breath. "How do you feel?"

"Like shit. What happened?"

I listened as he told me what he knew and what Maisie told him about what happened that night, ending with me taking a bullet to the shoulder and the Feds showing up.

"Sounds like I missed all the excitement."

He snorted and stepped inside the room, taking a seat on the edge of my bed. "You *were* the excitement, Peaches."

"What happened to Stranson?" I had to know if I could relax completely or if would spend the rest of my life looking over my shoulder. It was an uneasy thing to think about, being on the run with a gunshot wound.

"Cruz put two in him after he shot you. He's dead. I fucking froze, Peaches and I'm sorry."

"It's fine, Gunnar. At least Cruz is a better shot than Stranson. I'm still here. Still annoying the hell out of you, for a little while anyway."

"So you're still planning on leaving, huh?"

He sounded angry and maybe disappointed, but mostly angry.

"I can't stay here." Could I?

"Who says? What would you say if I asked you to stay?" Blue eyes were wide and full of hope, his full lips struggling not to smile.

"I don't know, Gunnar, are you asking me to stay?"

I was done with mixed messages. If Stranson was dead that meant I was still alive and still had a long life ahead of me. If he wanted an answer, he would have to ask the damn question.

This time he didn't fight the lip twitch. He let the smile spread until he was practically beaming. "Peaches, I want you to stay on Hardtail Ranch with me. And Maisie."

"Why? If this is some attempt at keeping me safe again, I don't need you to do all that."

"You are one damn stubborn woman, aren't you? I'm not asking you to stay to take care of you, but you can bet your sweet ass that I will protect you every damn day we're together. I want you to stay because I love you, Peaches."

He smiled at me, one of those sexy sweet smiles that hinted that maybe the boy next door might just rock your world.

"Somewhere along the way, I fell for you and your crazy. And I want you around all day. Everyday."

Damn. How did a girl respond to a declaration like that?

"Gunnar."

"Just think about it, Peaches. I know we didn't have the best start because I was a grumpy asshole, had a blind spot where you were concerned, and I nearly missed out on knowing you. Now that I know you, I want to know more. I want to erase that sadness from your eyes and replace it with pleasure. With joy. With love."

My eyes started to sting and no amount of blinking would relieve me. "You're determined to make me cry, aren't you?"

"No joking, Peaches. Not now."

He was right. "Fine. All that sounds good, Gunnar, but are you sure? It wasn't so long ago that you hated my guts and wanted me gone. Told me I was a good fuck but nothing more. You don't even trust me, so how can any of this work?"

"Because it will. Because I'm willing to be open minded about this shit. Plus, did you hear the whole part about me being in love with you?"

How could I not hear that? "It's the sweetest thing anyone has ever said to me, Gunnar. But I need you to be sure."

"I'm dead fucking certain, Peaches. Sounds like you're not though."

He was right. Maybe. "I love you, Gunnar. Even though I'm terrified you're going to wake up one day and remember how much you hate me, I love you. If I'm gonna try, then I need to know you're sure. That you love me and not who you want me to be."

"I love you, Peaches. All of you, from your dirty mouth to your big heart, the way you love Maisie. The way you're willing to help anyone, even grumpy assholes."

"Especially grumpy assholes," I corrected him, feeling my eyelids growing heavy. "I'll stay, but if you want me gone, just say the words. Okay?"

"I'm more likely to tie you to my bed than kick you off the ranch, but sure, I promise."

"To tie me to the bed? Sounds kinky." Even my words were starting to sound sleepy, and I reached up to stroke his chin, his jaw.

"Get better and I'll give you all the kink you can handle."

"The Barn Door? Off-hours? It's a fantasy of mine."

"Just say the word, and I'll fuck you as hard or as soft as you want. Whatever you want."

"I want you Gunnar. Just you." My lips curled into a smile as I drifted off to sleep, but I heard the sweetest words before sleep claimed me.

"Good, because I'm all yours, baby."

Epilogue

Gunnar ~ 6 Months Later

"Are you sure this is what you want to do today? There's still plenty of time to back out." Peaches had one leg hitched up on my hip, her naked body warm as it pressed against mine, a sultry smile on her full lips.

I palmed her ass, loving the husky way she laughed when I surprised her, and pulled her close so she could see what she was doing to me. "Don't try to wiggle out of it now. You've had six months to change your mind."

She tried to pull away, but I held her firmly. "I'm not changing my mind. I'm just giving you one last chance to change yours. Because I am a good fucking person."

"The best," I told her sarcastically. "Change my mind about making you mine completely? Not in a million fucking years, babe."

She smiled that sweet smile that was at such odds with her dangerous curves and sexy mouth, and the love I felt for Peaches swelled in my chest.

"Before the sun sets on this day, you will be my wife."

Wife.

It was a word I never thought would mean a damn thing to me, but it meant a hell of a lot. Ever since I'd gotten her to agree to marry me if we lasted six months, I'd been anxious to make her mine.

Today, I would.

"That sounds nice. Gunny has a wife," she sang in a voice that reminded me a little too much of Maisie. I tickled her, but my girl was tough and she didn't do ticklish, but she did wrap her hand around my cock.

"One more fuck as a single man?"

I grinned, but Peaches was already there, pushing me on my back and sliding down the length of my cock easily, proof she was hot and ready for me.

I gripped her hips hard, unable to tear my gaze away from the picture she made, natural and naked as she bounced on my cock, head thrown back in ecstasy.

"Peaches, babe."

She opened her eyes and smiled, putting her hands to my chest and riding me like she was on a mission, hard and fast while she held me in her gaze, transfixed. Hell, maybe I was spellbound because everything about the moment rushed to my nerve endings, sending fire and electricity over my skin until I could only feel what was happening.

"Gunnar. Oh fuck, yes! Gunnar!"

She rode, slow and deep and so fucking intense I felt the orgasm build starting with my toes.

"Gunnar."

She reached around and played with my balls while she rode my cock, and I was lost, body convulsing as the orgasm tore through me at her command. My body twitched and pulsed as my cock emptied into her body while she continued to ride, faster and harder, her fingers tangling in my hair as she brought her lips to mine, kissing me and moaning while she rode out her orgasm.

"Holy fuck, babe."

She let out a nervous laugh. "No shit, right? Now I can't wait to see how married people get it on."

I kissed her one last time before she pulled back with a sleepy smile.

"I know just the spot."

The moment I saw it I knew it would be perfect for a quiet moment alone, together.

"I can't wait," she purred and fell back against the bed, curling into my side. "But now I need sleep, it's my wedding day don'tcha know."

I smiled as she drifted off to sleep with a smile on her face. That was how I wanted to leave her anytime I had to, naked, smiling and satisfied. That was the plan. The goal.

TEMPTED

After spending way too long staring at the curve of her hip, I took a quick shower and got dressed. Today was special for a number of reasons, mostly because it was my wedding day. But there was another reason, and when I walked into the freshly painted Sin Room, where all Reckless Bastards business would be conducted, I smiled. Feeling right at home, once again.

The guys would all be here soon, pissed off and sleepy because of the early hour, especially when we'd all been up drinking until dawn, when I slipped away with Peaches to remind her why she wanted to marry me.

"Look at that goofy fucking grin. He's thinking about Peaches again," Cruz joked, leading the group with Slayer, Holden, Saint and Wheeler coming in behind him. "You didn't tie her to the bed, did you? We were joking about that."

"Yeah man, the authorities frown on that shit," Slayer joked and took a seat. "What's with the early morning meeting on your wedding day?"

"Glad you asked. I have some good news." That got everyone's attention because we'd been in a sort of limbo for the past few months, between Holden turning the ranch into a successful operation, and The Barn Door's membership doubling, life had been hectic.

Crazy hectic but good. Great, even.

"Business is doing well, which means we are all doing well."

There was close to a hundred mil in the accounts and I was happy to spread it among my brothers, handing them information for their personal club accounts.

"Before we get to this, we need to make it official."

"As long as there are no fucking robes or candles, I'm in," Holden groaned.

There may or may not have been a ceremony, but that was MC business. For Members only.

"It's my wedding day but I have a few gifts for you all."

"For Christ's sake man, it's y'all!" Holden flashed a smile and motioned for me to continue.

"Wheeler, you were the last to arrive, but you've proven that you're a killer second in command. Reckless Bastards, I present your Vice President, Wheeler!"

He strolled up to the front of the room, a cocky but distant smile in place as he took his patches and his vest. "Thanks, man."

"Slayer, because you look so sexy in your librarian glasses, you're Treasurer."

He stood and flipped his hair. "Worth all the sore throats," he joked but the man had a sense of occasion, hugging me tight before stepping back. "Thanks, man."

"Anytime, brother."

"Saint, you're the best to put in charge of weapons so I know you won't let us down as Sergeant at Arms." The freaked-out version of the kid was back, and I knew I'd have to talk to him soon. "Congratulations, brother."

"Thank you." His voice was quiet, barely audible, and he turned away before I could say another word.

"Holden with your big mouth and never ending chatter, you're our Communications Director."

His lips twitched in amusement, but his chest was puffed out a little more and his shoulders were a little broader as he walked up to get his patches.

"It's an honor," he said simply and shook my hand.

"Now you can open the envelopes," I told them and pulled out the heavy ass decanter of whiskey. "Let's drink to our success!"

We did. It didn't matter than it was just past ten in the morning, we drank like it was Saturday night until the decanter was nearly empty.

"Shit man, we gotta get you married," Holden said raising his glass in a toast.

"I'm getting married!"

Like it always did, the thought of marrying Peaches made me smile. "I'm going to fucking get married!"

"Oh shit, he's drunk. Peaches will kill us all," Wheeler joked as we all walked back to the main house, half-pissed. Before noon. As laid back as she was, Peaches had all the men more afraid of her than Martha. It was hilarious.

"She can't kill me, I'm her groom."

The back door smacked open, and Peaches glared at me, a big ass grin on her face. "Grooms are easy enough to find. Probably even a sober one."

"I'm sober," I insisted.

"I insist on a field sobriety test. Upstairs. Now." She turned and walked away but my body came to life and pulled me up the porch steps.

"Gotta go, guys."

They were all laughing. "Don't be late for the wedding," Slayer called out, amusement in his voice.

We cut it close, but we weren't late.

Not much, anyway. I fulfilled my promise and we were married by the time the sun sank behind the horizon.

"You're mine," I growled in her ear and twirled Peaches around the dance floor.

"And you are mine, Gunnar. Motherfuckin' mine."

Oh how I loved it when she got all sassy and possessive. "Always."

* * * *

~ THE END ~

Acknowledgements

Thank you so much for making my books a success! I appreciate all of you! Thanks to all of my beta readers, street teamers, ARC readers and Facebook fans. Y'all are THE BEST!

And a huge very special thanks to Jessie! I'm such a *hot mess, but without your keen sense of organization and skills, I'd be a burny fiery inferno of hot mess!! Thank you!

And a very special thanks to my editors (who sometimes have to work all through the night! *See HOT MESS above!) Thank you for making my words make sense.

Copyright © 2019 KB Winters and BookBoyfriends Publishing LLC

KB WINTERS

About The Author

KB Winters is a Wall Street Journal and USA Today Bestselling Author of steamy hot books about Bikers, Billionaires, Bad Boys and Badass Military Men. Just the way you like them. She has an addiction to caffeine, tattoos and hard-bodied alpha males. The men in her books are very sexy, protective and sometimes bossy, her ladies are…well…*bossier*!

Living in sunny Southern California, with her five kids and three fur babies, this embarrassingly hopeless romantic writes every chance she gets!

You can reach me at Facebook.com/kbwintersauthor and at kbwintersauthor@gmail.com

Copyright © 2019 KB Winters and BookBoyfriends Publishing LLC

Printed in Great Britain
by Amazon